KEE KEE, CUP & TOK

A NOVEL FOR CHILDREN

GW00713202

TOMMY FRANK O'CONNOR

ILLUSTRATED BY
LOUISE DUNNE

2004

First published in 2004 by Wynkin deWorde

Reissued by the author in 2012

A CIP catalogue record for this book is available from the British Library

ISBN: 0-9542607-8-3

Typeset by Patricia Hope, Skerries, Co. Dublin, Ireland
Design: Roger Derham / Design Direct, Galway, Ireland
Printed by Tralee Printing Works, Tralee, Co. Kerry, Ireland

ACKNOWLEDGEMENTS

I would like to thank Kathleen Browne, Kerry County Librarian, and her staff, for their invaluable support.

Thanks to Valerie Shortland for bringing out the best in Cup's story, and to Brenda and Roger Derham for their attention to detail in making this a quality production.

My special thanks to artist Louise Dunne for capturing the charm of Cup Little and her friends.

Thanks also to the management of The Cill Rialaig Project for facilitating me and so many artists and writers in providing that quiet and inspirational space in which to develop our work.

Tommy Frank O'Connor is a novelist, story writer, dramatist and poet living in Tralee, Co. Kerry, Ireland.

His stories and poetry have won many awards including a Francis MacManus Award, a Cecil Day Lewis Award, a CRANN Poetry Award and a shortlisting for the Hennessy Literary Awards.

Also by
Tommy Frank O'Connor

Novels
The Poacher's Apprentice
Marino Books 1994

Poetry Collections
Attic Warpipes
Bradshaw Books 2004

Meeting Mona Lisa
Doghouse 2011

Story Collection
Loose Head
Doghouse, 2004

Philosophical / Historical
PULSE –writings on Sliabh Lúachra
Doghouse, 2006

DEDICATION

For my grandchildren.

CHAPTER 1

DEEP IN THE FOREST

This was Cup Little's favourite part of the day. As she made her way into the forest on her way home from school, she sang a rhyme she'd made up for herself:

> *'A foster child is just on loan,*
> *My Mom and Dad are not my own.*
> *But if they're seeking love for free,*
> *They'll find it by adopting me.'*

In summer evenings she often climbed into a tree to watch the sunset over the bay and sit back against the trunk for a better view. She loved to see the sky full of strips of cloud gilded in a golden glow and the shimmering water reflecting the clouds giving them other shapes. She'd watch the sun going down for the night and always thought that, at that moment, it first gave everyone a glimpse of heaven.

A growl just ahead brought her back to the present. She stopped singing and crouched in the hiding place that old Mr Acorn had made for her. She stuck her fingers into her ears as she heard a chainsaw rip into a tree. She knew she should not be there but she just had to stay and pray that the saw would stop roaring; even a short pause to have a look at what it was doing might help. The saw would surely see that it was about to destroy the greatest pine tree in all the forest. She thought she could hear the tree crying. She waited and waited for it to stop but the ear-splitting noise just went on.

'How can this be happening to me?' Cup imagined the tree asking. Or - 'Why must I die while I still have so much work to do?' She thought she could hear the words in the wail of the tree. Cup knew it wasn't really the saw's fault; it was being forced to do this by the big rough hands of the man. His hands could almost break a branch off the old tree on their own, she thought.

A roost of rooks flew in circles high above their nests at the top of the tree. They flapped and swooped and cawed and made as much noise as they could. They too must be praying that something, somehow might choke the saw, thought Cup. And what about those creatures like squirrels and owls that had their homes in little tunnels and holes inside the tree trunk. They must be scared about what was happening too.

Cup huddled among the bushes and watched the top of the tree waving this way and that, over and back as if in a storm. But there wasn't even a breeze. The other trees in the forest dared not make a move in case they might draw attention to themselves.

The saw stopped. The old pine leaned to one side and quivered as if afraid of the big fall. Cup saw a wound, where the saw had been cutting, at the base of the tree. It opened wide. The tree swayed again. The wound closed and opened with each move as if it were a mouth trying to say something more.

Jack-the-Bear, as he was known, pushed three wedges of iron into the wound. Then he took a big sledgehammer and pounded these hard pieces of iron in. The old pine gave a groan and leaned further to the side. More hammering of wedges. *Crack!* Another pain shuddered in the tree. It tottered and waved its branches as if trying to stop itself from falling. A push, a grunt, a swear and a last big shove from Jack-the-Bear sent it crashing down, down all the way to the forest floor, landing close to Cup's hideaway.

From where she crouched, Cup could now see into the top branches of the old pine. Two nests made of brambles and lined with feathers had been torn apart in the fall and lay scattered on the ground. A smaller nest, made of what looked like mud, clung to branches farther along. Now she understood why the rooks were so upset. Three little rook chicks, barely out of their shells, had been thrown from their nest in the fall. They shook their black heads in surprise at being suddenly flung into briars and brambles. Grey eyelids hooded their eyes, like blindfolds.

Cup peeped between the branches. She was pleased to see Jack-the-Bear picking up his tools and leaving for home. When it was safe to move from her hiding place she crept towards the little chicks. She reached out to pick one up. It threw back its head and opened its beak wide, as if Cup was a vet wanting to examine its throat. Cup jumped in fright at the racket this started. The chick in her hand began to screech a noise that sounded like *'kee, kee. . . kee, kee'*. The other two then opened their beaks and joined in a rumpus of *kees*.

What can I do? The poor little things must be hungry, Cup thought. She looked up into the treetops, so high that they seemed to be half way to the fluffy clouds. The calls from the chicks brought the rooks back overhead. They looked like blackened anger, swirling about against the darkening sky.

'They're here; your little chicks are right here,' Cup shouted up and showed them the one in her hands. They flew down and perched on branches just above Cup's head.

'Caw!' one rook said.

'Caw, kaar, caw, kaar, caw,' they all repeated.

4

'I hear you . . . I hear you,' Cup shouted. 'If you'd made that much noise in the first place Jack-the-Bear might have gone away.' She pointed at the chicks.

Then she saw it. An egg sat on its broad end on a bed of moss that Mr Acorn had helped her make for an injured hare. Now I know what I must do, she thought. The rooks are afraid of me, so if I get back into my hiding place they can come down and take their little ones away to another nest. Cup placed the chick she held in her hand into the wispy grass beside the others, where they could be seen. Then she watched and waited. It was dusk and getting darker but she was not afraid. She was used to being out at night in the wilds. She felt safe here, away from what life outside the forest might try to do to her.

One of the rooks called out a rasping *'Caw!'*

The rest of the rookery answered by filling the air with *caws*.

Cup said nothing. That shiver she felt when people did not like her crawled through her again. An adult rook flew down and perched beside the fallen nests. Another followed, then two others. The chicks screeched *'kee, kee, kee, kee!'*

The rook beside the nest hopped onto the ground and seemed to take charge, as if it was the boss. A white patch joined the back of its bill to each eye. Other than that it was all black. It began to inspect the three small chicks, and then took a longer look at the chick that Cup had held in her hands. The chick screeched *'kee, kee, kee, kee'* and to her dismay Cup saw the rook shake its head before catching the little chick by its open, screeching beak and tossing it aside as if there was a bad smell from it. It landed within reach of Cup's hideaway.

Boss Rook went to the next two chicks and was greeted with more *kee kee's*. This time it behaved differently and let out a long *caw*, as if telling something to the others. It then dug its beak into the ground, pulled out a cluster of worms and dropped some into each chick's hungry beak. Boss Rook then walked around to inspect the egg. It stood looking at it and seemed to listen to it for a while, as if the egg were alive. It danced left and then right. Its feathers stood out on its neck like a cock getting ready for a fight.

'I know what you've been up to, you dirty little blue-face,' it seemed to say. Then Boss Rook pecked the shell hard with its beak, as if the little egg were to blame for their world crashing to the ground, before returning to the chicks it had just fed.

Boss Rook looked up and seemed to call to one of the other rooks perched near the nest on the fallen tree. It too hopped down onto the ground. After a dance and a few glances all around they both flew back up into the treetops, each with one of the chicks held carefully in its beak. Other rooks swooped over Cup and the rejected chick creating a chilling breeze before flying off, leaving a chick they did not want and an egg they did not like. The little chick was struggling to stand at the spot where Boss Rook had tossed it.

Fancy doing that to a little chick and an egg, Cup thought. She wondered about this, about nature's ways. Just then a rook-poo came down from the sky and landed on her head.

'Well thanks very much, you have great aim,' she yelled after the departing rooks.

It was getting darker; she wondered what she could do for the chick and egg. She certainly could not leave them; the chick would surely starve to death. There was probably another one in the egg, which would die as soon as it was born. She moved closer to them.

'I'm not a mother bird,' she said as she picked up the egg, 'but I'll think of something.' She tucked her T-shirt inside her jeans to make a nest, and placed the egg inside. She knew that eggs must be kept warm or they won't hatch.

By now the chick was *kee-ing* its head off, so she picked it up. It was trembling.

'Ah, you poor little thing, you're all frightened,' she said. She took off her knitted cap and placed the rook-chick inside. For food she picked insects off the bark of a tree and popped them into the open beak. It closed to swallow, but opened again and again for more.

'I don't think you know when you've had enough to eat,' Cup said, and smiled at the funny way the chick held its head.

Hiding an egg is easy, she thought, but what am I supposed to do with a baby rook that screeches at the slightest movement, as if the world was made to serve it? She began to walk towards home. Questions swirled around in her head. Yes, she thought as before, I'll find a way to make a home for these abandoned little things.

'And if we're to be a family I'd better call you something; so what name would you like?' Cup asked.

'*Kee, Kee,*' the chick screeched.

'*Kee-Kee!*' That's a funny name.

'*Kee, kee ... kee, kee,*' the chick insisted.

'All right, all right,' Cup whispered. 'But you'd better keep quiet. I'll have to take you home to my space in the loft and hide you until you grow some feathers and learn to fly. Mrs Hewitt would be even less pleased than your own mother at the sight of you.'

'*Kee,*' Kee-Kee croaked quietly, and cocked its head as if looking for more information about this strange creature called Mrs Hewitt.

'She's my mother; well not really. She's my foster mother ... a kind of mother for the moment, like I am for you, if you know what I mean.' Cup felt a slight movement inside her cap, as if Kee-Kee wanted to know more.

'I know; you're not supposed to talk to strangers, is that it? Well I'm Cup,' she said.

Kee-Kee stirred but did not make a sound.

'It is a strange name, I suppose. But that's what I was called when I was young like you. One morning a woman opened the front door of her house to take in her carton of milk. There was no milk, only a cardboard shoe-box with an empty cup on top of it. She opened the box, thinking that someone might have hidden the milk carton in it. And there I was, stuffed into a leg warmer inside the shoe-box with this knitted cap. So she took the box and the cup into her house. When the people from the Social Services came to take me away the woman had already given me the name *Cup*.'

'Kee,' the little chick said as it stirred in the cap.

'You want to know more?'

'Kee,' the chick whispered.

'Well, I was told that the cup had a map of little cracks on it and that it had lost its handle.'

The chick seemed to be happy with that. It settled quietly in Cup's cap.

Cup crept up the ladder into her loft space and placed her cap under her quilt. Then she went back down to the kitchen to find supper for herself and Kee-Kee, thinking:

> *Little birdie in my hat,*
> *Good job we don't have a cat.*
> *He would grab you just for fun*
> *And eat you, little one!*

CHAPTER 2

A BAG FOR A NEST

Downstairs Mrs Hewitt was not having a good day. The welcome home was what Cup had come to expect when she was late getting back from the forest.

'Where have you been? Do you have any idea of the time? And what about your homework?' Mrs Hewitt yelled as she caught Cup by the shoulders and shook her.

'My homework is fine; I did it while Teacher was checking work in school,' Cup replied with a shiver.

'How dare you answer me back.' Mrs Hewitt grabbed two fists of Cup's long hair. 'Oh this is filthy,' she added, and tied the hair into a knot.

'May I make some supper now?' Cup asked.

Mrs Hewitt said nothing, only huffed and wrung her dirty

hands. She cleaned them on her shirt and returned to her needlework.

A smile would crack the lonesome face Mrs Hewitt had worn these past few weeks, thought Cup. She again tried to think of a way to cheer her up. She'd spoken with Mr Hewitt about it when he was home at the weekend. "It will pass; it always does", he'd said, hopefully.

When Cup bent over to see what was in the fridge she felt the egg rolling around in her T-shirt. She had forgotten that it was there and was glad that Mrs Hewitt hadn't spotted it.

Back in the loft she shared her cheese, corned beef and bread with Kee-Kee, and put some aside for the chick's breakfast. She placed the egg near Kee-Kee in her cap, took off her clothes and got into a nightdress. Shampoo and a shower would be nice, she thought, but there wasn't any in this house. So she untied the knot out of her hair, dipped it for a rinse in the basin and dried it with her dress.

She put her cap, with Kee-Kee and the egg still in it, into an old boot of Mr Hewitt's she'd made into a doll's cot. When they were nice and comfy she took them into the bunk with her for the night. Underneath the duvet she drew herself into a ball, and prayed that somehow she would think of a way to keep the nest in her cap safe while she was at school. There would be no point in saving these little creatures only to find them killed by a cat, or by a sparrow hawk.

She was about to fall asleep when one thought jumped up

over all the others. 'You're my birthday present,' she said as she lifted up the duvet for a peep; 'I was ten last week and nobody remembered only myself. Now we can have our birthdays together.' With that special thought she smiled and fell asleep.

Cup woke up as the early rays of the sun peeped through her skylight window. It was just as well because, when she drew back the duvet and looked in her cap, she saw that bits of the shell had fallen away from the top of the egg.

Kee-Kee said, *'kee kee'* and opened its beak as wide as it could go.

Cup fed it breakfast from the leftovers of last night's supper. Then she saw that the sides of the egg had also cracked, and were moving in and out, as if breathing. She picked up the egg. More bits of the shell fell off. She picked at a piece. It came away as soon as she touched it. Soon she had peeled away all the other pieces and, all of a sudden as if by magic, there was a tiny chick wriggling in her hand. It tried to stand and move its head. Cup shaped her fingers around it like a little nest. For a long moment all she could do was feel the thrill of this little thing coming alive in her hand. She held it against her face. The chick's tiny heart beat out a message of love to Cup.

'And I love you too.' Cup kissed it and whispered. She then took another, closer look. Like Kee-Kee, its head was too big for its body and it had no feathers. Yet it was

different. The head and beak were not the same shape or colour as Kee-Kee's. The chick moved again

'This is a strange place isn't it, funny face?'

The chick held its damp head to one side.

'It's called the world,' Cup said. 'It's a really big place. You'll see when you learn to fly up into that great open sky,' Cup whispered and kissed the chick again. She then went down the ladder, found a few crumbs and scraps and brought them back up to make bird-breakfast.

Kee-Kee seemed to be happy and full so Cup took a crumb and offered it to the new chick. For a moment it did nothing, then Cup realised that it couldn't see yet. She then opened its beak and placed the crumb inside. The chick swallowed and opened its beak wide for more.

Cup hoped that Mrs Hewitt would keep to her usual 'bad time' habit of not getting up until after Cup had left for school. She thought of a plan to hide the chicks while she was in the classroom, and to get them in and out of the house without Mrs Hewitt noticing. There was plenty of string under her bunk so she tied her schoolbooks with that and placed the chicks in her school bag.

Down in the kitchen she found more food scraps and put them in her bag.

Where am I going to put you two while I'm at school? Cup wondered to herself as she walked along the edge of the forest. After about a mile she crossed a road into the fields near the school and stopped to look around. She was still quite early. Off to her right she saw the perfect hideaway. There was a copse of yew trees and bushes only a field away from the gable end of the school. She ran across the field and into the copse and looked up into the branches of a leaning tree. Then she climbed as high as she could. There she opened the bag, fed the chicks again, closed the bag and wound the strap around a branch.

'I'll be back at lunch time,' she promised as she climbed down to the ground.

'Where's your school bag?' Teacher asked when she saw Cup's bundle.

'I left it up a tree, Miss,' Cup said, and handed up her homework exercises. Teacher was about to say something when a few children in the class sniggered.

'What are you laughing at? I don't see anything funny,' Teacher said.

All morning Cup wondered why, when she wanted it to go fast, time seemed to travel on the back of a snail. She looked up at the classroom clock. It was only 10.00, and there were two-and-a-half more hours to lunch-break. She thought she heard someone calling her name.

'Good heavens, child, your mind must be a 1,000 miles away,' Teacher exclaimed.

Not that far; just at the end of the field, Cup smiled at the thought, and said nothing.

'I must have called you ten times and you just kept on gazing out that window.'

'Sorry, Miss, I was thinking of my schoolbag,' Cup said.

'Your schoolbag, as you call it, mightn't be worth much, but it's a lot better than that piece of twine!' Teacher went on.

Some of the class turned to look at Cup, and giggled. A few stuck out their tongues; others held their noses. She had seen it all so many times and that cold shiver still ran through her. But they were still in the classroom and couldn't gang up on her like in the schoolyard or on the way home.

Her schoolbag was indeed a bit different; one she'd made herself from Mr Hewitt's old jeans after he threw them away. That was one good thing about the orphanage she had lived in, she thought; you could learn to do all sorts of things just by looking at how older people did them. Some of them would even show you how to sew or cook or make things, if they saw that you were interested. She liked to have enough space in her bag for the things she found by the roadside or in the forest as she made her way to and from school. Last week she had found a piece of electric cable. She took it home and made it into a skipping rope. Some of the other children, especially the boys, thought it was cool.

'I don't think it's even a little bit funny,' Cup heard

Teacher say, who didn't realise that Cup was smiling at the thought of her chicks and their droppings in one of those beautiful leather bags some of the other children had.

She settled down and listened as Teacher explained the new section on mathematics. They worked their way through the examples. Cup's mind drifted away again while she was waiting for others to catch up on the exercises.

At last it was lunchtime. Cup raced around to the gable end of the school and checked that no one was watching. Nobody there only a pair of magpies. She ran at the wall and jumped as high as she could. Her fingers gripped the top. She hauled herself over. The cattle in the field didn't seem to notice.

CHAPTER 3

BAD HAIR AND BAD TIMES

Summer was happening all around her and the scents of flowers and buds filled the air. Butterflies hovered among the grasses and wild flowers. The warm sun danced in the speckled greens of the trees and bushes. Honeybees were too busy to notice anything. Cup looked behind. Sometimes the farmer let his bull into the field with the cattle, so she ran along by the ditch until she reached the corner. If the bull were to attack she could then easily escape across the ditch or up a tree.

She reached the copse of yew trees. A jump, a pull and a short climb brought her level with her schoolbag. Everything was so quiet. Cup lifted the flap of the bag.

'Kee, kee ... kee, kee,' went Kee-Kee.

The chick hatched from the egg made a gurgle of sounds and finished with something that sounded like *'Tok'*.

'You haven't touched the scraps I left for you,' Cup said. She picked the chicks up and snuggled them against her face. Then she fed them bits of bread and bacon rind and meat loaf. It's like dropping the food into tiny flower vases, Cup thought. The top opens; you put in food. The top closes; swallow food, then opens wide for more. She gathered what was left into the palm of her hand and held it near Kee-Kee. The chick just threw back its head and opened its beak again.

'Don't you have a brain in your head at all?' Cup asked, as she wondered why Kee-Kee wouldn't pick some food for itself.

She gathered up the younger chick and held the food towards it. It didn't throw back its head, but moved it in a way that showed it seemed to be aware of something. After feeding it, Cup placed it in the other half of the bag, covered it with the flap and tied it back into place. She had just reached the ground when she heard the school bell. Only two minutes to get across the field and into line.

Sitting at her desk in the classroom Cup realised that she had forgotten about lunch for herself. She hadn't brought any from home so she had nothing to eat or drink. Her head felt light, as if there was a balloon inside it wanting to float away. After the race across the field, her mouth felt dry. Her face was hot and flushed and her hair was tossed.

'About little chicks, Miss ... are they able to see when they come out of their shells?' she asked when she saw a little bit of irritation in the way Teacher was looking at her.

'Not at first, no; a few days ... a few weeks, depending on the chick. Why do you ask?' Teacher stood beside her.

'I was just wondering, and I thought you'd be the best one to ask,' Cup looked up at her. 'May I get some water please?' she asked as Teacher walked back to her desk.

'Just after your lunch! Oh go on, and run a comb through your hair when you're out there,' Teacher said.

I must think of a name for my new chick, she thought later while Teacher handed back the homework.

'I can't understand how your homework is always so neat and perfect,' Teacher said as she handed Cup her copybooks. 'When did you wash your hair last, or do you ever look in a mirror?' she went on.

'When it rains,' Cup whispered.

'You rely on the rain to wash your hair!' Teacher exclaimed as if wanting everyone to hear.

'The river too, Miss.' Cup just looked at her books and said no more. She didn't want to tell that there was no door in the Hewitt's bathroom and that the soap in there was so hard it would strip the nails off your fingers. A smile flickered at the thought that no one would dare go in there if Mrs Hewitt was in the bath. Cup had her own way of having a shower; no need to turn on or off a tap.

Each pair of eyes in the class was looking at her. A few were friendly. Most peered at her as they might look at a monkey in a cage or a fox caught in a trap; a wild thing that might snarl and bite them at any moment before tearing herself free and slinking away to her den.

Then she thought of the birds and all the wild animals. They didn't use soap or shampoo, and seemed to manage perfectly well without bathrooms. Her mind drifted away again to the forest, to her chicks. She thought of the chicks coming out of their shells into a great big world. Perhaps that's why they cannot see for a while afterwards, they need to get a sense of the place, she said to herself; if they could see too soon their other senses wouldn't learn how to work. Then her own story of having been left on a doorstep came back to her: coming out of a shoe-box like a chick out of its shell. Cup wondered if the chicks would remember any of their first impressions of the world; she certainly could not.

Teacher clapped her hands, wrote the exercise for the night's homework on the board, and waited while the children copied it down. After writing in the questions, Cup quickly worked out the answers and also wrote them in her copybook.

When the final bell sounded she found that it was easy to run around to the gable end while everyone else went in the opposite direction onto the road. She ran at the wall, took a leap and pulled herself over. I'm getting good at this, she thought as she raced along the edge of the field. She looked back at the bull as she climbed up the slope of the tree trunk. He didn't seem to be thinking of anything. The schoolbag hung on the branch where she had left it. Kee-Kee went *'kee, kee ... kee, kee'* when Cup opened the flap. She picked up the other chick; it was weak and not able to stand.

What do I do when someone gets weak? Cup asked herself as she hurried down the tree with the chicks in her bag. Water, that's it; I must find water.

Cup ran towards the stream at the end of the next field. There she stood Kee-Kee in the water. She held the other chick in her hand in the water. Then she had an idea. She opened its beak open with one hand and splashed some water into it with the other. Little eyes blinked; Cup waited. The chick shook its head and opened its beak for more.

After more splashing it said something like *'Tok'*. It was a sharp, hard sound like whacking a block of wood with a stick.

'Tok?' Cup asked.

'Tok,' the chick said, again sitting into her hand.

'I'd better get you some food,' Cup said.

She could not wait until they got home. It was too far, more than a mile away. She had learned that birds like worms. Cup also knew that worms liked the soft soil near streams. She turned over a flat stone. Four worms tried to wriggle into the ground. Cup grabbed them before they could get away.

Kee-Kee opened its beak wide like a tiny waste bin. She dropped a worm in.

'And what am I to call you?' she said to the younger chick. 'I think it should be something you can say yourself,' she added, and teased its beak with a worm.

The chick said *'Tok'*.

'That's it, I suppose. It's the only thing you seem to say.' Cup said as she placed the chick in the water at the edge of the stream. 'You're <u>Tok</u>,' she added as it flopped about in the water. Tok shook its head in surprise and repeated its name, as if it was swearing.

'Happy Birthday to you, Tok' Cup sang as she lifted it from the water and fed it a birthday worm.

Kee-Kee screeched out its name.

'All right, no need to be jealous. I'm not forgetting you,' Cup said, turning over another flat stone and surprising a handful of worms.

She fed Tok and Kee-Kee their fill of wriggly worms until they seemed to be happy. Then she thought about going home. First she put the chicks into her cap and the cap into one side of her bag. She then untied her bundle of books and fitted them into the other side of the bag. With a sigh she set off for home.

When Cup got home Mrs Hewitt having a 'bad time'. Mr Hewitt had hoped that his wife would not get into a state like that again: the last time it happened was at the new year; she had been all right for almost six months since then.

Cup peeped into the lounge. Mrs Hewitt was sprawled on the sofa. She had forgotten to take off her nightdress before pulling on her day clothes. The buttons of her cardigan that were closed were in the wrong buttonholes.

'I'm home,' Cup said.

Mrs Hewitt shook her head and made shapes with her face until she got her eyes to work. She opened her mouth and made a face of angry wrinkles.

'You,' she spluttered, pointing a half-empty bottle of

wine at Cup but then seemed to forget what she wanted to say. She waved the bottle around for a while before thinking better of it and drinking the wine from it instead.

'I'll make a pot of tea,' Cup said, and went to the kitchen.

Cup had mixed feelings about Mrs Hewitt's state; when she went into her 'bad times' it could last anywhere from two weeks to two months and this upset her. On the other hand Mrs Hewitt would not notice two chicks of the forest coming in and out of the house in a school bag. With any luck, Cup thought, Kee-Kee and Tok could live outdoors in a few weeks and might even have learned to fly by the time Mrs Hewitt ran out of wine.

A 'bad time' for Mrs Hewitt was a bad time for Cup. She did not seem to know the difference between night and day. She could scream at Cup at 3.00 in the morning, shouting "you've stolen my dinner" or "you're hiding my bottle". Worse still, she sometimes tried to climb the ladder up to the loft and fell. Then Cup would have to get up to coax and help her back to bed. Mr Hewitt was little help as he was rarely there. He worked as a commercial traveller and was away from home from Monday to Friday each week. In any event he was in no hurry back to his wife when she was going through her 'bad times'. He was tired of those 'bad times'.

CHAPTER 4

LEARNING TO FLY

A month went by and the chicks thrived and grew feathers. Cup discovered that Kee-Kee was a *rook*, a female; she was just the same as all the others in the forest. By the rough feathers around Tok's neck, and his willingness to eat almost anything, Cup knew that he had to be a *raven*, a male - from his colouring. By now he was bigger than Kee-Kee and would spread his wings as if to show that they too were much wider.

'It's time you two learned to fly,' Cup said one Saturday morning. 'Sorry I can't show you how to do it,' she added, but she had a plan.

While watching birds and animals in the forest Cup had noticed how they trained their young. Time didn't seem to matter; mommy bird would fly a little way from the nest and coax each chick to follow. She'd do the same again; waiting while the chicks got their heads around the idea. Then they'd try to make short flights from the nest.

Cup decided to climb into a tree with her chicks. There she stood them on branches and watched as they weaved and staggered a little; Kee-Kee almost tumbled off. Soon however they learned to keep their balance, and knew that this place was right for them. Kee-Kee shook her head and said something like *'kee-aw'*. She liked the sound of it and said it again. Tok opened out his wings in that proud way of his and danced on the branch. He said his name and *'craw'*, and added a few more rattling sounds. Every time he moved, the sun played a sheen of blue and purple along his feathers.

Cup watched them. They looked at her in between glances at the great big world from half-way up this oak tree. She knew that they would soon fly away. They would meet others of their own kind. Nature created them to build nests and set up families of their own.

The thought made her a little sad. She knew that sad things happen for a reason and being upset about them doesn't make them any better. Up there on the oak branch her chicks seemed to grow before her very eyes. They were chicks no longer. With spreading wings and shining feathers, they wanted to soar up to the sky; they were now young birds.

Another thought came to brighten her mood. Mr Hewitt

would not be home this weekend so all day today nobody would know, or care, where she was. And tomorrow was Sunday. After church, she would prepare something to eat for Mrs Hewitt; something simple, like broth. Because she was in one of her 'bad times', Cup would probably have to feed her too; she'd dip bread into the broth and get her to eat it. But after that she would be free and she'd have the rest of the day just for herself and her chicks.

Cup liked being free; free to roam in the forest; free to choose her friends. The thought of being one of those children who always had to tell their parents who they were playing with made her smile. School was the same; they didn't want you to be free: Do this, do that ...

'You two don't need all those rules to guide you,' Cup whispered as she looked at Kee-Kee and Tok. She was amazed at the amount of food they were now eating. Here the forest had ways of looking after its own. Bigger birds and animals killed smaller ones. After eating what they needed they left the rest for others. It became part of the forest.

Cup guessed that Tok would be the first to fly. He was stronger and, with wings that wide, he would hardly come to any harm. Indeed with wings like Tok's Cup could almost fly away herself, she thought. Cup picked up Tok and climbed down. At the other side of the clearing left by a fallen tree she climbed an elm until she was higher up than Kee-Kee on the oak.

Kee-Kee kee'd and kee-awed.

'Fly to Kee-Kee,' Cup said as she threw Tok high in the air. He seemed surprised to find himself up there with nothing to stand on. After a moment's confusion he spread his wings and flapped and flapped until he crashed into the oak and fell. He flapped his wings again and landed on the branch beside Kee-Kee. Tok looked across at Cup. He tokked and cawed as if giving out to Cup for throwing him away from her.

'Back to Cup; come on back here to me,' Cup said as she clapped her hands and held them out to them.

The chicks looked at each other and then at Cup as if expecting *her* to fly across to them. She climbed down until she was lower than they were, and called to them again.

They leaned forward and danced sideways, but did not open their wings.

'Ah come on, what have you got wings for?' Cup said. Food, she thought, they'll come for food and remembered she had seen a dead rabbit near the oak tree. She climbed to the ground, ran across to the base of the oak, grabbed the rabbit and climbed back up the elm. She had always thought of elm trees as twisted and ugly. Up close they were so interesting. Their branches didn't seem to care which way they were supposed to go. So they went left, then right, up and down. Just to be sure they sent out smaller branches to do the same. A racket from another tree brought her back to the moment.

'Lunch time; come and get it.' She held up the rabbit.

Kee-Kee said *kee-caw*. Tok said everything he could think of. She swung the rabbit back and forth to make sure they knew what it was. Again they flapped and danced. Cup could see that they wanted to get across to her but they did not seem to know how. She flapped her arms. They looked puzzled, as if wondering where her wings were hiding.

'Well if you two think I'm climbing up there to collect you, you can forget it,' she yelled across at them. To show that she was serious she threw the rabbit onto the ground and climbed down after it. She could see that the birds' attention was focussed on each move she made, so she picked up the rabbit and waved it at them again.

'Lunch time, see you,' she said, and walked away.

Such a racket from the oak tree. It was like a bird meeting, with both speaking at the same time.

Cup listened, but forced herself not to look back. 'You'll just have to use your heads,' she said, and kept on walking and swinging the rabbit. She had learned that birds and animals and fishes were not as intelligent as people, but she also knew from her experience of the forest that some of them were very clever. They knew what they had to do to live. She remembered how the eels swim for hundreds of miles to the Sargasso Sea to do whatever they had to do there. Salmon and swallows and all sorts of creatures did amazing things. They could swim through oceans and rivers, or fly through storm and rain for days and weeks. So there was no reason why a young rook and raven couldn't fly down from a tree.

'If you don't hurry, it's rabbit sandwiches and stew for Mrs Hewitt,' Cup said but still did not look back.

She remembered animal stories she'd read in the orphanage library and nature programmes on television on Saturday mornings or on wet Sunday afternoons. She loved to watch as creatures of fur and feather played or searched for food.

Suddenly Tok landed on her shoulder and said *Tok*. He patted her head before tucking his wings away. Cup stopped in surprise. She was about to take him down and kiss him but then thought otherwise. She shouldn't make a fuss. Just regard it as ordinary and natural, and maybe Kee-Kee would follow.

Tok picked at her hair. 'Ouch!' she said, and remembered that he must be hungry. He was probably trying to ask her what she was doing with the rabbit, she thought. She dropped the rabbit on the ground, and watched. She did not have long to wait. Tok flew off her shoulder and landed in a stagger beside the rabbit. Soon he was pecking at it with his beak. It was as if the feast was all for him.

'Sorry, Mrs Hewitt; you're out of luck for the rabbit sandwiches,' Cup said; 'don't give up on the stew though,' she added, and allowed herself a quick peep back at the oak tree just as Kee-Kee flew out from its branches. She flew up and down and sideways. Her wings flapped so fast you'd think she was imitating a humming bird. She looked down at Cup as if wondering what to do next. Tok continued with his lunch. For a moment Kee-Kee seemed to stand straight up in the air before plopping to the ground beside Tok.

Then another strange thing happened. Kee-Kee stood and danced around. She seemed to be saying things to Tok, but not eating any of the rabbit. She didn't even attempt to pick at it. Tok took a look at her, pulled off a chunk of meat with his beak and dropped it beside her.

Kee-Kee picked at it. She dropped it on the ground and had a good look at it and then at Tok. She then decided that if it was good enough for Tok it must be all right for hers, and began to eat. She chewed as hard as she could but her beak was not as strong as Tok's. She dropped the piece of meat on the ground. After taking another look at it and at Tok, she scratched it with her claws. Then she took it in her beak and tried again.

Cup now had another problem. Her young birds were becoming independent. They still had to master the art of flying but, as this was natural for them, it would only take a few days. It would take a little longer for them to learn how to find food, and she'd help for as long as necessary. But how could she keep them safe at night? Indeed she wondered how they'd behave themselves from now on while she was at school.

Then she remembered that school holidays were due the next week. She would have time to prepare Kee-Kee and Tok to survive in their world. The little birds hopped across and looked up at her. Now that their tummies were full it was as if they wanted her to tell them a story.

Cup picked up the birds.

'All right, my little friends. I know all about you so it's only fair that you should know my story.' She knelt on the warm grass and sat back on her heels. The birds stood before her, turning their heads from side to side. 'You know,' she said, smiling at the birds. 'I nearly found myself living in the city. My first home outside the orphanage was with the Moore's. They lived in a row of houses all tied together like a string of sausages. Not a tree to be seen anywhere; little bits of garden that hardly knew what the sun looked like.

There were two boys so the family wanted a sister. The boys' idea of play was to watch video films and play video games. They'd eat sweets and drink out of cans all day long. Bulges of fat hung off them from their necks to their heels. The only other game they knew was to sneak into my room at night and pull me out of bed.

I didn't like it. You wouldn't, would you? So I ran away. It was winter. For ten days I lived on raw vegetables and scraps of bread. I don't have feathers like you so I felt cold, especially at night. A woman saw me picking scraps from the waste of her market stall. She took me home. There I had a bubble bath, a change of clothes and a yummy dinner before Social Services took me back to the orphanage.

Before Christmas that year they gave me to another family. Like the Moore's they needed a sister, or so they said. There were three boys, two older than I, and one younger by a month.

They lived beside a park where the boys played football. Girls were not allowed to play there, or so the boys said. In a way it was hard to blame them; they were the worst footballers of all time. If the two of you perched on a rope they couldn't kick you off it.

So I went out and played there anyway. It was that or dust and scrub indoors yet again. Someone got upset. Social Services decided that I was not for normal fostering. Funny thing about that is no one ever spoke to me about what was supposed to be normal.

I'm not saying the orphanage was so bad. Lovely people of all ages would come in sometimes and give us a talk. Do you know that there's some good in the worst of us? That's what those people used to say, and they may be right. Some said that if a bad person finds a good friend, things tend to get better. When the good person does something kind it makes the bad one think again.

Anyway, then Mr Hewitt applied to Social Services for someone as a companion for his wife. She suffered from loneliness while he was away working, he said. They had no children, and he thought one might be of help. Social Services knew that no child would want to live so far away from a town or village. The Hewitt's were far from everything, except the forest. Then Social Services thought of me. That was two years ago last Christmas.

So here I am. And you two'll have flying stories to tell in a few days. So now I think it's time to get back to see how Mrs Hewitt is doing.'

CHAPTER 5

SUMMER HOLIDAYS

On the last day of school before the holidays Teacher had prizes and treats for the class. There were bowls of crisps, peanuts and sweets to be shared by everybody. Cup dipped her hand in a bowl and took a few peanuts. She noticed the other children didn't want to share with her. She decided she'd try the same with a bowl of crisps. Soon she had each bowl all to herself.

Then it came to the prizes: Most Improved Girl; Most Improved Boy; Best at Music, and so on. Cup clapped her hands and was happy for each of the winners.

'Best at Mathematics – Cup Little.' She went to Teacher at the front of the class but was not given a prize. Instead Teacher held her back while she called out Cup's name for best at each subject, along with best attendance. She then reached under the table and handed Cup a leather schoolbag. Some children clapped their hands. Others were not so kind.

'There are things in the bag for you, child. Please use them,' Teacher whispered.

'But this is your own new bag, Miss,' Cup said.

'It's yours now, Cup. You need it more than I do.'

Cup walked back to her seat. Class was over. They were now free to go home. Cup put her new bag on the desk and reached down to pick up her old one. She thought of the short while since Kee-Kee and Tok nested there as chicks. Now they wouldn't fit in the bag. When she looked back up her new bag was gone. She looked towards to door. Two girls held up the bag and beckoned her to follow them.

She saw that there were still some peanuts and crisps that had not been eaten.

'May I have these please, Miss,' she asked.

Teacher nodded and went on packing books into cardboard boxes. Cup tipped the contents into her old bag, then gathered all the bowls and left them in a stack on a desk. She noticed Teacher dabbing tears from her eyes, and wondered. 'Happy holidays, Teacher,' Cup said.

'Well thank you, Cup, and I hope you'll always be happy,' Teacher hugged and kissed her.

Outside, a group of girls and boys gathered around her. Two of the bigger ones took her by the arms and ran her out the gateway and down the road. There they pushed her against a thorny hedge and showed her what they'd done to her new bag. The straps were pulled off. Every stitch was ripped out. They hadn't been able to tear the leather.

Then they emptied out the packet that was inside the bag. A bottle of shampoo, soap, toothbrush and toothpaste, a bottle of scent, bubble bath, and a large and small towel fell out. The children danced on top of them shouting and laughing.

She watched them, five girls and two boys all much bigger than herself. Her arms felt sore from the rough grip when they dragged her here. Her skin felt like it was turning to ice. She thought of saying something; asking them to leave her alone but when she opened her mouth a scream came out, a sharp, long, loud shriek. Once it got going it seemed to take on a mind of its own; Cup didn't need to draw a breath.

The children drew back and looked at each other. Without saying a word they bent down and began to throw things at Cup: the torn bag, plastic bottles, and soap. Then it was their turn to scream.

A black raven dived at them out of the sky, followed by a young rook. The raven beat at the children with his wings. He pulled the hair bands off the girls' heads. The rook flew in mad circles overhead and cawed as if she needed to be heard at the other side of the world. The screaming children ran away.

'Tok, Kee-Kee, please don't,' Cup called out. Then, she began to weep. Tears just burst out of her without moan or sound. It was like those lonely nights in the orphanage; then she was not allowed to speak to anybody after lights out.

She fell to her knees. To find breath she had to open her mouth and gasp. It was as if her lungs emptied faster than she could fill them. She gasped harder. Her thoughts raced around in her head.

Then she heard swishy noises. Tok had landed beside her. Kee-Kee was making another crash landing. She moved towards them on her hands and knees, and held out her hands. Then she remembered the nuts and crisps in her old bag. She dipped in and gave them their reward. Tok then hopped onto her shoulder. Kee-Kee looked at the things on the ground.

'You're so good; so clever. How did you know what to do?' She took Tok off her shoulder and dried her face on his feathers.

Tok said *'tok, tok'*, and something that sounded like *'ava, ava.'* Kee-Kee picked at the white soap that lay on the ground, didn't like the taste and ran to Cup to clean her beak.

'We'd better gather up these things,' Cup said, and piled the bottles and battered wash things into her old bag. Then she folded the leather of the new bag and tied it with the straps the children had pulled off.

'First of all, another little treat for you two, just to say thanks,' Cup said and beckoned them to follow her. Tok hopped onto her shoulder, and Kee-Kee somehow managed to land on her head. Again she took the birds to the soft mud beside the stream in the forest. Cup bent her knees to lift a stone. The birds hopped onto the ground.

Kee-Kee was first to dive at the worms when the stone roof of their world came off. The little rook drove her bill into the soft muddy bed, pulled out a worm and swallowed it. She did this a few more times watched by Cup and Tok. Tok then scratched moss from a rotting tree stump and had a feast of creepy crawly things.

Cup did not feel like going home and spoiling all this fun. Her chicks were now feathered and learning very fast. Only a few weeks ago they couldn't feed themselves, she thought.

Tok had mastered flying in just over a few days and was not at all fussy about what he ate. The evening before he'd dropped a dead mouse on her head when Cup came into the forest. He then exchanged toks and caws and babbles with Kee-Kee, as if they had planned it all and the game had worked.

Kee-Kee was learning also. She was still smaller than Tok and her feathers were just black; without any sheen of blue. Her wings were not going to be anything like the spread of Tok's. Though she could now fly quite well she was still useless at landing. She'd almost touch the ground, then somersault and make the landing. It was like her head knew what she wanted but her wings thought they knew better. So she seemed happy to perch on the oak tree and let Tok soar into the air whenever he wished.

Summer was a great time for bathing in the river. Cup would strip off, dive in and swim around in the pool. After a few days of this she noticed that she had an audience. Cup and Kee-Kee perched on an overhanging branch. It seemed to her that they wanted to share the fun she was having. She knew that they could never swim because they had no webs between their claws. Still they might like to have a wash, so she went to the edge of the pool and climbed onto a ledge underneath the branch.

'Come here to me,' she said and held up her hands to them both.

Tok flapped his wings, and made a swirl of noises. He nearly knocked Kee-Kee off the branch as he rose in the air and landed on Cup's hand.

'Come on, Kee-Kee,' Cup said, and Tok repeated similar sounds.

Kee-Kee flapped her wings even more than Tok had done. She rose into the air, but flew wide of Cup's hand on her way down. She almost landed in the water. Then up into the air she rose again as if she was afraid the water was boiling. Cup reached out and managed to grab her, then climbed down towards the pool.

She waded into the water. To free one of her hands Cup placed Tok on her arm beside Kee-Kee. She was surprised at how heavy they had become. With her free hand she splashed water on herself and then on the birds. Kee-Kee opened her beak, just like when she was a chick waiting to be fed. Tok shook himself and shrugged and flapped, sending a spray of water over all of them.

By now it was much too risky to walk through the house and up the ladder to the loft carrying two birds with beaks full of noisy questions. They would certainly not be the type of company Mrs Hewitt would appreciate. Indeed she would probably greet them by trying to wring their necks. Cup didn't want them to end up in a stew so she thought of a plan.

'Stay up there until I call you,' she told them as they flew into a pine tree at the back of the house. Cup ran into the house and up to the loft. There she jumped on the chest of drawers under her skylight, reached up and opened it. She clung on to the ledge and pulled herself up so that she could see the birds.

'I'm in here if you want me,' she called out to them.

A few minutes later Tok landed on the ledge and looked in. Kee-Kee joined him, and they seemed to be having a chat about whether or not they'd come into the room. Then Cup saw that if they were to roost in the room it would probably be on the rafters or the clothes-line. Then there would be a mess of bird droppings each morning.

There must be somewhere safe outside where they can roost, she thought. She went out to the shed and searched among the cobwebs and years of dust. An old bicycle met her hand. It was so rusty there was no trace of whatever colour it had been. Screams and whelps of excitement swooped from behind her. Tok landed on her shoulder. Kee-Kee tried to do the same on the other shoulder, but missed. Her somersault landed her on the handlebars of the bicycle instead. Cup laughed. Tok threw up his head and sounded as if he was laughing too. Kee-Kee shook herself as if to say, "I'll show you, yet".

'What do you think you're doing?' Mrs Hewitt yelled from the back door. 'Come and do something useful.'

'I'll take the wheels off this and make a tree-house for you two,' Cup said, quietly to the birds.

Cup placed Tok beside Kee-Kee on the handlebars of the old bicycle and walked back to the house. If only I could get away from all of this, she wished. Then she smiled and ran past Mrs Hewitt. If only I could fly – fly up into the treetops and soar over the forest like Tok and Kee-Kee, she thought.

Yes, if I could sprout wings and fly, she wished again. She could see herself up there in the sky, her wings spread wide and soaring like Tok, going wherever the flow of air might take them. She'd look down and watch her shadow swoop along the ground.

Cup thought of all the advice she'd been given in the orphanage; about being the friend who'd make a difference in someone's life. Could she make a difference in Mrs Hewitt's life ... make her happy? Cup wondered.

CHAPTER 6

THE CLOTHESLINE

It was almost a week later that Mrs Hewitt suddenly realised that Cup was on summer holidays.

'Jobs, child; can you not see the whole house must be cleaned up and down,' she croaked through a throat that didn't sound like her own.

'You're not well, are you, Mrs Hewitt?' Cup asked.

Mrs Hewitt blinked in surprise. She opened and closed the wrinkles on her face in a grimace.

'I'll make you some tea,' Cup offered, and went to the kitchen. What if Mrs Hewitt could have this dream of flying; of soaring like Tok, Cup wondered, as she filled the kettle.

'You're not trying to wangle your way out of the cleaning, I hope?' Mrs Hewitt croaked.

'I'll start after I've made the tea,' She called back from the kitchen.

'I'll leave the pot with you and you can pour for yourself,' Cup said as she took another look at the woman who was meant to be her foster-mother. Her eyes rimmed by a glimmer of tears, Mrs Hewitt looked back at her.

Cup started by collecting up the bottles, dirty cups and glasses. These were scattered everywhere; in the kitchen, lounge, upstairs in the bathroom and in the Hewitts' bedroom. She also gathered up a trail of clothes for washing. She wondered what could have brought Mrs Hewitt to this state; to the 'bad times'. The poor woman surely wanted to be happy. Oh dear, Cup thought, the more Mrs Hewitt drank from those wine bottles, the more she awoke further away from happiness.

When Cup had separated the wash into two piles she looked around for washing powder. There was none, so she took some of that hard soap from the bathroom and grated it over the clothes. Then she loaded the first pile into the tub of the washing machine. She added a little bubble bath for scent, and set the machine to full wash.

Outside the window Tok pecked at the glass and flapped his wings. Kee-Kee landed on Tok's back for a better view into the kitchen.

'Can't you see I'm busy?' Cup said as she tried to get the vacuum cleaner to work. Then she realised that it was too

full of dust and anything else it might have picked up. The cure for this would be to change the bag, take out the full one and put in a new one. There was no point in searching for a new bag; Cup knew there wasn't any. She hoped that the tape she'd fixed on the old one after she last emptied it was still good.

'I'm off to empty the vacuum,' she called to Mrs Hewitt.

Outside she was joined by the birds as she tried to empty the bag. Only a little bit of dust came out, so she made a hook out of a piece of wire and poked it into the bag. Soon she had an array of bottle corks and tops, bits of old carpet, safety pins, Mrs Hewitt's missing nylon stockings, Mr Hewitt's tie, a comb with gaps in its teeth, and more broken glass and cups than she thought possible. The sticky tape holding the old bag together still clung on. There were no holes or cracks.

Back inside the house the machine sucked and roared as if wanting to fill its tummy as fast as it could. The first wash finished as she switched off the vacuum. This was her chance to escape. She pulled the clothes from the machine, gave each item a good shake and threw it in a basket. Then she loaded the second lot into the machine, added soap and bubble bath, reset it and went out to the clothes-line.

She could not see the birds anywhere, nor did she call them. The clothes had to be pinned on the line. After that she could play.

'Kee-Kee! Tok!' She called when she was ready. For a while there was no answer. Soon Kee-Kee arrived with a carrot in her beak. She dropped it at Cup's feet, like a waitress serving a choice meal. Then Tok zoomed in and dropped a bit of mouldy bread. Tok looked at Cup as if to say – 'you try this, it's yummy'.

Kee-Kee flew onto Cup's shoulder and offered her a taste of the carrot.

'It's ever so kind of you both, but I'll take my chances with Mrs Hewitt,' Cup said. She looked for somewhere to sit, and settled on an upturned bucket. There she waited for the birds to have their meal. As she watched them she wondered how they could be so alike and yet so different.

Kee-Kee was turning into a little boss, just like her mother. Soon she too would have that white patch from her bill to her eyes. This would show that she was grown up.

Tok was getting so strong, always picking things up in his talons. A few days earlier he had dropped a large bone beside her in the forest.

'Where are you now Cup? Lazing about as usual!' Mrs Hewitt's voice rattled from the door. In her mind's eye Cup could see Mrs Hewitt starring as Witch in the school play.

People can be so unfair to each other, Cup thought as she went back into the house. Why can't they think about what they do, how they can hurt even with words? She looked up into the Mrs Hewitt's eyes. They looked sad. Cup wondered what she had been like as a little girl: what she liked doing; what made her laugh, if she'd had any special friends; like Kee-Kee and Tok.

'I'll hang out the second wash. Is there anything else, Mrs Hewitt?'

'Just mind you don't overload the clothes-line,' the woman warned.

Cup had been thinking about that very subject. The clothes-line didn't have a thing on it for weeks; then it had to carry all the wash at once. It seemed to have been hanging there for years. Cup took a good look at it and decided it must be as old as Mrs Hewitt's wrinkles.

In fact Cup liked washing time in this house. It nearly always meant that Mrs Hewitt was rising out of the 'bad time'. Cup saw it as the sun rising from darkness to brighten up a new morning. It meant also that Mr Hewitt would come back to the house again; that the place would feel more like home.

Now all of the clothes were on the line: down one side of the garden, across the bottom and up the other side.

Cup hoped for a few hours without rain. She could then get them all back in the house and maybe get Mrs Hewitt to help with the ironing. Just then Kee-Kee hovered over the line and landed on a sheet. The line swung as she tried to balance. It swung and then snapped where it was tied to a tree in the corner.

Kee-Kee took fright and flew off to join Tok on a nearby apple tree. There they watched as Cup gathered up the clothes. She put them back in the big basket, took the end of the line and climbed the tree. Tok flew down and perched beside her. Cup looked at the piece of rope tied around the tree. If she could undo the knots there would be enough to make a new joining. She held the loose broken end towards Tok.

'You must hold this for me while I untie the knots here,' she said.

'Tok', Tok said, as if meaning "I beg your pardon?"

Cup put the rope in her mouth to show him what she meant. She held the rope up to him again. He took it in his beak. Cup began pulling at the knots. They were a little too hard for her fingers. Tok looked to where Kee-Kee was watching, as if to ask her to get off her perch and do something. She got the message and flew down.

Again Cup pulled at the knots. Then Kee-Kee started to peck and pull with her beak but wasn't able to get them loose. Tok began to dance on the branch. Kee-Kee hopped across to him. Cup watched in wonder as he gave Kee-Kee the rope to hold. Tok then attacked the knots. Cup watched those hard feathers standing out on his neck as if he was in a fight with the knots. I must remember not to argue with you, she thought. He pulled and tore at those knots until they were loose enough for Cup to undo them. Soon the three of them had fixed the line.

CHAPTER 7

HOME COOKING

Next morning Cup was first into the kitchen as usual. She noticed a hat and coat hanging in the hallway. They had to belong to Mr Hewitt, she knew. She looked through the cupboards for food but there was none.

'Good morning, Cup. Busy, I see,' Mr Hewitt appeared from nowhere.

'Nice to see you, sir, but I'm afraid there's nothing for your breakfast.'

'Or yours either, I can see.'

'So why don't you give Mrs Hewitt more money?' Cup asked.

Mr Hewitt stopped. For a moment Cup thought she saw a look of anger on his face. But she'd said what she had wanted to say for some time. She'd said it and she decided to let it be said.

'Of course it isn't that simple; giving Mrs Hewitt more money does not always mean that there will be any more food to eat,' he sighed.

'Perhaps you could buy the food yourself, sir,' Cup suggested.

'Or perhaps you'd like to go to new foster parents?' Mr Hewitt asked calmly. He didn't smile; neither was he angry.

'No, I don't think so,' Cup said, and tried to remain as calm as Mr Hewitt.

Of course she'd often wished for a new home, but not now. What would happen with her friends Tok and Kee-Kee? What if she found herself with fussy parents like some of the children's in school? Parents who'd want to know everything about what she was doing: her previous family wouldn't allow her out to play football. The one before that forced her to eat everything on her plate.

There would be no more long days in the forest. No more looking at the world from a treetop. No more living the way she wanted to. And now there was Mrs Hewitt. The poor thing seemed to be trapped in a black sadness. There had to be a way of getting her to see how good the world could be. Perhaps if she became interested in something it might bring a buzz into her life, Cup thought.

'So you're happy to go without breakfast, and the lord

only knows what else?' Mr Hewitt took Cup by the hand.

'Of course not; I'm hungry, but I'll find something somewhere,' Cup said.

'The Social Services Inspector wouldn't like to hear you saying that.'

'Why? Why should any Inspector want to know?' Cup tried to stay calm, and wondered why people who knew nothing about her or her feelings should still decide how and where she should live.

'Because we never know when one of them might visit,' Mr Hewitt said quietly.

They stood looking at each other. Cup remembered the Social Services and Childcare people she'd met. Most of them were kind. They wanted each child to feel part of a family.

'Then we'd better get some food in,' Cup pleaded: 'food and other things. We'll show them how good we are. You bring me to the shops in Cureen; I know what's needed,' she added.

Mr Hewitt agreed to give it a try. In the car he asked if she was happy that she'd been sent to live with them.

'I've never been happier,' Cup shrugged.

'Even though the nearest neighbour is half-a-mile away?' He creased his forehead and looked at her.

'The forest is full of life; friends that don't ask questions, they'll do me for neighbours.'

'So you wouldn't like to go back into care?' Mr Hewitt asked as he wheeled the trolley around the supermarket.

Back into care! Cup shivered and put all the things she could think of into the shopping trolley. She even got Mr Hewitt to invest in a new microwave oven which was on special offer, telling him how quick it was for cooking Then she added plain and wholemeal flour, breadsoda, buttermilk and dried fruit, and everything required to make homemade bread.

She so wanted to make this; remembering the aroma of the baking from the kitchen when she was in the orphanage and how much she wanted to eat the bread and scones, but rarely got any. That homemade touch was one of the things children in care missed most so Cup had read all about the making and baking of bread. She learned it and went over and over it again in her mind. One day, she promised herself, she'd have a home of her own; then she'd never again long for the flavour and taste that made her mouth water. She'd bake everything, and share it with everybody.

'Does anyone from Social Services visit the school?' Mr Hewitt asked on the way home. He sounded concerned.

'I've never seen any. The schools Inspector was in our class before the holidays. I got on fine with her,' Cup assured him.

'I see.' He seemed to be looking into his mind as well as at the road. 'Cup? Do they ever advise you in school about anything?' he then asked.

'Apart from lessons?'

'Yes. Coping with life and advice like that,' he said.

'Oh! That stuff. *Civics* they call it.' Cup nodded.

'Tell me about it.'

'No big deal. Don't do this; don't do that,' she said.

'And you think it doesn't apply to you?'

'Some of it maybe; life skills stuff,' she shrugged.

'Life skills?' He looked at her with a look of amusement.

'Ah you know – decisions about right and wrong, how we come to be born, caring for the sick and poor . . . and so on. I don't need school for that.' She watched him thinking about this for a while.

'The world isn't all nice, you know,' he said.

'Tell me about it!'

'I worry about you sometimes, Cup. Always going off into the forest on your own and that.

'No need to worry about me,' Cup said, 'I think I'd know an evil eye if I saw one. Teacher told us about that.'

Back home Cup helped Mr Hewitt to get his wife out of bed and then went down to the kitchen. She set the oven to heat while she mixed the flour and other ingredients in buttermilk. Soon two brown cakes and two of mixed fruit were soon ready for the oven. Changing her mind she picked up one of the fruit loaves. I'll make scones out of this one,

she thought, before rolling it flat. She then took a cup and shaped off a dozen scones before moulding the leftover scraps into another scone. Maybe that's where the baker's dozen idea came from, she thought.

Tok landed on the windowsill. Kee-Kee joined him as Cup turned the first lot of bread in the oven. They were looking at the fruit scones and thinking of breakfast.

'I know what you're up to, you two. As soon as my back is turned you'll be in like a flash to steal my scones. They're not for you.'

Cup ran outside, pointed to the apple tree and told them not to come closer than that. 'Up there with you now,' she ordered. They looked at her and then at the tree. 'Up on the apple tree, I said. Come on, I don't have all day.' She watched as they reluctantly flew from the kitchen window to the apple tree.

Mrs Hewitt arrived downstairs fully dressed and smelling clean. The grey in her face had turned to brown and her eyes looked brighter. Cup gave her an apron. She looped the top over Mrs Hewitt's neck and tied the strings behind her back.

'Now you see; you look like you've been up all morning baking,' Cup laughed.

'Why would that matter?' Mrs Hewitt asked.

'Oh! I don't know.' At that point Mr Hewitt walked into the kitchen. Cup looked at him. 'Maybe if the people from Social Services ever came to the house, they would like the smell of fresh bread. The smell of love,' she added.

Mrs Hewitt looked at Cup in a way that Cup had not noticed before, her eyes flickering, looking like she might cry. She sat down but said nothing. Cup then filled a bowl with muesli, topped it up with milk and gave it to her. Mr Hewitt smiled as he busied himself setting up the new microwave oven.

CHAPTER 8

GOOD AND BAD

Not since the first week of this fostering could Cup remember the three of them sitting down to breakfast at the same time. They would sometimes be together for lunch or dinner, depending on the time of day it was ready. Cup would never forget their first dinner together. The meat went into the oven as a leg of lamb; it came out as a cinder with a bone sticking out each end. Some days they would have no meals at all.

Just as she remembered this she suddenly smelt burning bread. Rushing to the oven she took out the two bread cakes and set them on the window-sill to cool. She then placed the mixed fruit cake and scones in the hot oven and returned to the table. Sitting down, she noticed that a pair of teardrops had made tracks down on each side of Mrs Hewitt's nose.

'Ah poor Mrs Hewitt, why are you sad?' Cup placed an arm around her shoulder.

Mr Hewitt said nothing.

'Life can be so strange,' Mrs Hewitt blinked. She opened her mouth to say something to her husband, but nothing came out.

Cup looked at Mr Hewitt. She hoped he could read the pleading in her face.

'While I'm home why don't I take you to see the doctor, dear?' He looked at his wife and smiled at Cup.

'I'm perfectly fine, thanks all the same.' Mrs Hewitt's answer was half-hearted.

Something was different though, Cup thought, it was as if Mrs Hewitt wanted help; wanted to leave the 'bad times' behind.

After a good deal of pleading from Mr Hewitt, she finally agreed to go.

Cup ran out into the yard. She found that old piece of electric cable she used as a skipping rope. While she skipped she sang her rhyme:

'A foster child is just on loan,
This Mom and Dad are not my own.
But if they're seeking love for free,
They'll find it by adopting me.'

She noticed that Tok had landed on the ground in front of her. He jumped in and hopped over the rope in time with her own skipping. She didn't have to look for Kee-Kee. She flapped and hopped up and down the apple tree, cawing as if telling the story of what was happening. Cup got the aroma of the fruit cake and scones and ran back into the kitchen.

'You must remind me how to make these,' Mrs Hewitt said as she took them from the oven.

'Let's go, you two,' Cup said after the Hewitt's had left to go and see the doctor. The birds flew ahead of her as she ran towards the forest.

Then suddenly she heard it! Jack-the-Bear was back. Cup could hear his chainsaw growling in the distance. The roar of the saw grew louder as she got nearer. It sounded as if it had a bad pain. Tok and Kee-Kee flew just above her head. She felt that if she reached up and grabbed their legs they could fly her along with them. But Kee-Kee somersaulted and swooped down in front of her. She stopped running. The frightened rook clung to her, her little heart thumping in fear inside her feathers.

'My poor little Kee-Kee; I'll always be your friend, your mammy if that's what you want,' Cup promised. Tok flew to the spot on the oak tree where he had first begun to fly. Cup put Kee-Kee inside her T-shirt as she walked towards the roar of the saw. She was just in time to see the

last cut. Jack-the-Bear had reduced the great old pine tree to a heap of logs.

Tok perched on a branch above him. He looked across at where Cup and Kee-Kee crouched, as if wondering what to do. Kee-Kee peeped out from inside Cup's T-shirt. She rubbed her head to Cup's neck and clung to the inside of her T-shirt with her claws.

'Oh you poor thing,' Cup said. 'Now I know what's wrong with you. You remember that something bad happened the last time you heard this noise.' She cuddled Kee-Kee to her and stroked the sheen of her feathers.

She ran across to Jack-the-Bear and climbed on the logs to stand as tall as he.

'Why are you doing this?' she asked.

'Cause that's what my boss asks me to do, little Miss.' His beard bristled as he looked at Cup and then at Kee-Kee's head peeping out over the collar of her T-shirt.

'Your boss asked you to cut down this great pine?'

'This one for now, yes.' He narrowed his eyes and spat at her feet.

'For now!' she shouted. 'You mean you'll be cutting down more trees?'

'Who's to stop me?' With an ugly laugh he pulled at the cord and the chainsaw motor spluttered to life. He pressed a button on the handle and the saw roared in her face.

The sound filled Cup's ears to bursting. She fell back

off the logs. Tok swooped and picked off Jack-the-Bear's knitted hat. He beat at Tok with the saw. Tok hovered over him and dropped the hat onto the spinning blade. In a few seconds the hat became a thousand bits of wool.

'If I catch you I'll stuff you in a bottle, you little rascal,' he yelled at Cup as she ran from the forest.

Back home Cup told the Hewitt's what had happened.

'You picked an argument with a man in the forest! With a chainsaw in his hands!' Mrs Hewitt exclaimed. She looked to her husband to say more.

'You really need to be careful; remember those lessons from school,' he said.

'But I had my friends with me.' Cup pointed to the window.

'Birds! You're for the birds,' Mrs Hewitt scolded.

Sometimes a thought tingles when it's right, thought Cup; when a little heart beats inside it like a chick in the palm of your hand. Cup smiled at Mrs Hewitt's renewed interest in what was going on around her. All she needed now was to get her involved in what was happening outdoors.

Summer stretched its long sunny days of July into August. Each night before she went to bed Cup prayed that nobody would ever take her away from here. Tok and Kee-Kee roosted in the little tree house she'd made with the bicycle wheels and some long pieces of wood near the top of the

Scots fir beyond her window. The birds always seemed to know when she was awake; they flew out of their tree house and perched near her open window to greet her.

During August they flew further and further away and did not come back to her as often as before. Cup knew that they would soon find mates of their own and begin to build nests. Or maybe they'd agree that one of them would stay in the tree house. They would do whatever they wanted to do. Nobody from Social Services or anywhere else would tell them what they should do. Nature would guide them.

Mr Hewitt went off to work early each Monday morning and returned on Friday evening. One week while he was away a man came and fitted a door to the bathroom. It wasn't a new door, but it had a lock, and coloured glass panels that you could not see through, making the light match the panels.

Things were getting better. Cup found a tangle of old fishing line in the river. It was just what she needed to stitch her leather schoolbag back together.

Mrs Hewitt finished the course of tablets that the doctor had given her. They seemed to have worked and with Cup's help she took a new interest in cooking, and also bought some new clothes.

'Why don't you get your hair done? It would make you feel even better,' Cup suggested.

'Look who's talking,' Mrs Hewitt joked. But she did visit the hairdresser and came home looking ten years younger.

Soon it was time to return to school. Cup took Mr Hewitt shopping on the Saturday before school reopened. She wanted to go back to school as fresh as the blossoms on the trees. As Mr Hewitt wheeled the trolley Cup filled it with shampoo and soap and all those items on the shopping list she'd made out with Mrs Hewitt.

'There'll be no need for you to be up in the morning before I go to school,' Cup advised Mrs Hewitt. To emphasise the point she brought her tea and toast before she left.

Cup wondered what the birds would do when they saw her going towards the school. She walked towards the forest and then turned onto the pathway through the fields. Off they flew into the forest. When she got to the tree where she'd hidden them as chicks she smiled at how quickly they'd grown. The leather of her new schoolbag still smelled fresh, and she'd also bought a new pen, pencil and copybooks on Saturday's shopping trip.

The first morning back at school was full of stories: where families had gone on holidays; what new friends they'd made in other countries; the new things they'd bought. But some things hadn't changed.

Even though Cup was neat and clean and her hair was no longer a mop in need of a comb, some of the children still held their noses when they looked at her. She reached into her bag. She took another copybook and turned to the middle pages. There she drew the faces of those holding their noses and sticking out their tongues.

Their new teacher explained the first maths problem of the year. It was called long division. He wrote an example on the board and then gave them a test with three problems to solve.

Cup wrote these into the front page of the copybook. Just like short division, only with bigger numbers, she thought as she finished each one. Then she returned to the middle of the copybook to complete her drawings. She did not notice the teacher standing beside her desk.

He picked up her copybook. After looking at it he asked her why she hadn't done her sums. She showed him the first page where she had done them. He looked at the sums, then at her while he raised his eyebrows and nodded.

'Is this what you see when these children look at you?' he asked as he handed back her copybook.

'Yes, sir,' Cup said. 'That's what I see. And welcome to our class.'

'And your name again?'

'Cup; Cup Little, sir,' she said.

'And these sums; how did you manage to get them right so fast?'

'They're easy, sir; they're only about how many times one number fits into another,' Cup looked up at him.

The new teacher stood there, thoughts creasing his forehead. Then, with a sigh, he looked at the work of the others in the class. Cup got a feeling of goodness from him, like she'd got from Mr Hewitt, Mr Acorn and good people in the orphanage.

After the last bell rang everybody gathered their stuff into their bags. The school emptied as if it was on fire. Some ran to climb on buses, others to get into family cars. Cup looked around but could not see Kee-Kee or Tok. She ran to the far gable end of the school and back again. She was alone. She climbed over the wall and ran. Still no sign of her birds.

Soon she was in the forest. Kee-Kee came to meet her. She landed on her shoulder, pecked at her hair and flew ahead. Cup got the feeling that there was something wrong. She ran after Kee-Kee. The young rook guided her through a part of the forest where she'd never been before.

Briars and undergrowth slowed Cup down. Kee-Kee perched on a low branch and waited. At last Cup could see the problem. Three men with hard yellow hats were measuring a tree. Tok was perched on the top looking down on them. They seemed to be too busy to notice him. Kee-Kee flew up to join him.

The undergrowth allowed Cup to move closer without being seen. It was high, so she didn't have to crouch. She moved slowly and carefully. She didn't want to step on a dry twig or make a noise that would alert the men to her presence. Kee-Kee flew across to her. The men took no notice. They were talking.

Cup heard the words: 'furniture', 'chairs' and 'boats'. One of the men moved back almost to where she stood. She watched him point a camera at the tree and take a few photographs. Tok did not move.

Cup waited until the men moved away. She went across and examined the tree. The birds joined her for a look. It was an elm and seemed to be in perfect health. The bark was almost silver white with rough brown marks lined into it. The trunk was thick and strong. She could see where the men had drilled a hole in it near the ground. Just above the hole the number 67 was stamped on the bark.

'Does this mean they have their eyes on 66 other trees as well?' Cup asked the birds. There was no answer so she took the question home to Mrs Hewitt.

'Really Cup, you must try to keep your nose out of other people's affairs,' Mrs Hewitt said as she lobbed an overdone pork chop onto each of their plates. She still hadn't got the hang of cooking properly.

'Kee-Kee and Tok wouldn't agree with you; it was they told me about it.'

'They told you about it?' Mrs Hewitt's eyebrows wrinkled into her forehead.

'In their own way. They're really clever, you know . . . like twins; what one won't think of the other one will.' Cup took a bite of her chop. It tasted better than it looked. Outside the window she saw a line of fresh washing flapping in the breeze. She noticed the classy table manners of Mrs Hewitt; the way she held her knife and fork, her upright poise on the chair.

'Mrs Hewitt.'

'Yes, Cup?'

'Would you tell me a story, please?'

'Me tell you a story! Haven't you got lots of stories yourself . . . new ones every day?'

'What I mean is . . . your own story, about when you were young, where you grew up, what it was like . . . you know what I mean.' Cup finished her meal and laid her knife and fork side by side.

'I suppose it's only fair, you should know something about me,' began Mrs Hewitt. 'I was born here almost 40 years ago. We lived on a big estate then, over 300 acres. We were wealthy then. My mother died when I was very young, so I was passed around among the family. I went to several schools, then to finishing school in Switzerland. When I came home from there something had changed. All that was left was this house, that yard out there and a few scrubby acres around it.' She paused.

Cup could see she was near to tears.

'What happened?' Cup asked.

'My father was a gambler, and other things too. The land

and whatever stock was left went to pay his debts.' She stood up from the table.

'It's okay; leave those, I'll wash up,' Cup said. She wanted to know more but Mrs Hewitt went upstairs. Cup knew she would have to wait awhile before Mrs Hewitt would fill in the gaps in her story.

But this conversation had opened a window of thought for Cup. While Mrs Hewitt might not remember much about her mother she must have some image or picture of her somewhere. And her father, good or not so good, was still alive in her head.

Cup wondered about her own parents; if they were alive or dead; if they were together, or if they ever thought about her.

CHAPTER 9

CHRISTMAS SNOW

Weeks went by. Halloween came and went. Cup checked the forest every day but nobody came near the trees.

The days shortened into Christmas. Kee-Kee came to meet her each day on her way home from school. Tok met her only when she came into the forest. He'd glide towards her like a jet plane coming in to land. Sometimes he brought a gift held in his claws: a golf ball, a rusty car jack, bottles, and all sorts of things. Then he'd land on her shoulder, always her left shoulder, and rub her hair with his right wing before folding it away. Cup would raise her face to him and he'd caress it with his head. He was now three or four times the size of Kee-Kee. She wondered how such a big bird could move so smoothly, without making a sound.

The weather became dry and frosty. Cup loved it. She would put on her coat and race across the field. On Christmas Eve the snow came. Cup was asleep in her bunk in the loft. Sometime in the night she thought she heard a noise. She sat up and rubbed her eyes. The noise came from the skylight; hard tapping sounds.

It had to be Tok, she knew. She peered up. Though she couldn't see through the glass she felt that there was something different about this night. It was as if it were dressed in a veil. She pulled her bunk across under the skylight, stood on tiptoes and opened it.

A shower of snow swirled around her. Tok stood on the edge of the frame and peered down at her. Kee-Kee then landed beside him. For a moment they looked at Cup and she looked up at them. The birds seemed to be discussing something.

'Would you like to come in? You poor dears, you must be freezing!' Cup held her hands towards them. Kee-Kee hopped down onto her right shoulder. Tok tokked and cackled and danced around the frame of the skylight. Cup and Kee-Kee looked up at him. Kee-Kee cawed something to him. He paused, then danced and cackled some more as snowflakes floated past him.

'You'd better make up your mind because I have to close this,' Cup reached up and caught the lever. Tok squeezed himself through the opening and floated onto her left shoulder. He was dripping wet. Cup quickly closed the skylight. The birds hopped onto the bunk and Tok shook the water from his feathers.

'Well thanks very much!' Cup said as she looked at her wet nightdress and duvet. The snow that had fallen on her and her bunk melted to water. A closer look showed that only the top of her duvet and pillow were wet. She turned over the pillow and got a dry nightdress from the hot-press. While she was doing this the birds flew onto the edge of the old dressing table where they had roosted as chicks.

Cup went down to the kitchen. Unlike the time when she brought Kee-Kee here in her cap, and Tok was still in his shell, there was now plenty of food. Mrs Hewitt had come shopping with Cup and Mr Hewitt. Though they had a shopping list Mrs Hewitt examined most of the goods on the shelves. She hadn't been into town for ages, so she sent Cup to get another trolley for all the things she wanted to buy. Even if they were snowed in for a month there would be enough to eat.

In the kitchen Cup chopped up an apple into a cereal bowl, added in scraps of skin from the cooked ham and a slice of brown bread she'd baked that day. She poured milk into a saucer and left it for the kitten Mr Hewitt had got his wife for Christmas. Then she drew some water into another bowl and climbed carefully back into the loft. With this feast

Tok and Kee-Kee did not need an invitation to an early taste of Christmas breakfast.

'Do those birds really speak to you? I know they don't speak words like we do, but you seem to know what you're saying to each other,' Mrs Hewitt asked on one of those lazy evenings after Christmas, as she stroked the kitten purring on her lap.

Cup had once again gone to the forest in daylight and returned by moonlight, hungry but full of stories.

'It could be that we know what we're thinking, especially if one of us is in danger,' Cup said.

'Amazing,' Mrs Hewitt said.

'Wouldn't you like to come to the forest with me? Tomorrow maybe?' Cup took hold of Mrs Hewitt's hand. The woman shook her head, and smiled when Cup squeezed her fingers.

'Remember when we went shopping, all the great things you saw. The forest is even more exciting,' Cup urged.

'I don't know,' she said, with that ask-me-again look.

'There's a pathway through the field, and it's lovely there.' Cup danced around the floor.

'I've been wondering what makes you want to go there all the time,' she said, and then agreed to go the next day; just for a few minutes.

'I've never worn trousers in my life,' Mrs Hewitt protested the next morning. After bringing her breakfast in bed, Cup told her she'd made up some food in a basket. 'We can go early and have a picnic in the forest,' she said.

'But we'll freeze,' Mrs Hewitt shivered.

'Not if you wear the clothes I've laid out for you,' Cup said. Mrs Hewitt picked up her husband's old corduroy trousers and looked from them to Cup.

'I hope nobody sees me,' she said, as she got dressed.

Tok and Kee-Kee seemed to pick up the excitement as Cup and Mrs Hewitt set out on their journey. They carried the picnic basket between them. Mrs Hewitt moved slowly at first, as if not sure that she wanted to be out. Soon she moved along freely. As they got nearer the forest they began to swing the basket between them.

It was like the Christmas shopping all over again. In the forest Mrs Hewitt stopped and gazed at everything.

'Can you smell the different scents?' Cup whispered.

Mrs Hewitt closed her eyes and stood still as she did so.

'It's wintertime now. Most of the place is sound asleep, but you can still get a scent of cones, and fir, and fern. Can you smell a squirrel's nest?' Cup went on.

Tok and Kee-Kee perched on a branch to have a look. Mrs Hewitt opened her eyes and sat down on the picnic basket. The birds flew around among the trees and landed side by side on the same branch. For a while nobody stirred.

'What do you do when you come here?' Mrs Hewitt asked.

'Have you ever climbed a tree?' Cup asked ignoring the question.

Though Mrs Hewitt was seated on the basket, Cup had to look up into her eyes.

'Climb a tree!' She put her hands to her face.

'When you were young like me, you must have?'

'I wasn't allowed to.' Mrs Hewitt slowly shook her head.

'The world is so different from up there: the sunrise; sunsets, everything.'

'You must tell me about them sometime.'

'Oh yes! Yes, I will!' Cup promised.

They strolled further into the forest, pausing to feel the different types of bark on the trees. Little birds like wrens and robins flitted and played among the twigs. Mrs Hewitt let go her handle of the basket when a hare sprang from a briar patch beside them. Cup thought of her old friend Mr Acorn who had helped her build her hideaway. She remembered her first meeting with him as if it were yesterday.

Walking in the forest one day she suddenly got a whiff of smoke - tobacco smoke. Someone was smoking a pipe. Cup recognised that smell. The swarm of midges surrounding her suddenly disappeared as she approached the smoke. Then she saw him: an old man sitting on a log, busy puffing clouds of smoke from his pipe. His eyes were closed. He didn't see her at first but he seemed to sense her presence.

'Good day, Sir,' she greeted him.

'And a very good day to you, my dear,' he replied, his eyes twinkling as he leaned forward to have a closer look at her.

'What's your name, Sir?' she asked.

'Folks around here call me Acorn,' he told her.

'Is that smoke magic?' she asked.

'Magic smoke? Jeepers Creepers!' The old man said with a wheezy laugh. He coughed until his eyes watered. 'Ah now I know what you mean,' he said when he saw her looking back at the midges. 'Midges don't like smoke, that's for sure, but let me tell you another secret: they love the scent of fear,' he said, pointing at her with the stem of his pipe.

'How can they smell fear?' she asked.

'There's nature for you. You don't have to understand everything to know that that's the way it is.' He coughed. After a pause he explained that the scent of fear attracted creatures as small as midges and as big as tigers, or even sharks. They'd attack whatever gave off the scent.

'Why?' she asked.

'It tastes better that way,' he said with a wink.

Cup sighed, thinking of old Mr Acorn. After that first day she used to meet him in the forest as often as possible. they would sit in the hideaway and watch the birds and animals. Then one day he said he was going away and not coming back and that he wanted Cup to look after the forest. She promised she would.

Cup told her all about old Mr Acorn and how he had asked that she look after the forest when he was gone.

'Old Mr Acorn! My goodness, is he still alive?' Mrs Hewitt sounded amazed. 'You know, he seemed *old* when I was young like you,' she added.

After lunch they left food scraps for the birds, and tidied everything else into the basket. Mrs Hewitt felt tired. 'I haven't had so much fresh air in years,' she said as they walked back home.

'We must do this again soon, but you're back at school in a few days,' Mrs Hewitt sighed.

'Sure I go through there on my way to school and again on my way home,' Cup clapped her hands.

'All that long way around,' she said, 'but I can see now why you'd want to do that.'

Chapter 10

The Storm

The weather changed from dry and frosty to wet and cold after the school holidays but a few weeks later they had snow again. This lasted for three more weeks. Mrs Hewitt wouldn't dream of going out in such weather. The snow was followed by a fortnight of hail and sleet. Then came a Friday late in March when the wind became stormy.

Mrs Hewitt awoke as Cup placed her tea and toast on her bedside locker.

'You can't go to school on a day like this!' she said, looking out the window.

'I'll be fine, honest,' Cup assured her.

'You'll be blown away. The wind could pick you up and toss you in front of a truck.' Mrs Hewitt grabbed her arm.

'I'm not going by road, remember,' Cup said.

She kissed Mrs Hewitt goodbye and ran through the fields, into the forest and out into fields again. True for Mrs Hewitt, she thought, the wind did pick her up in the fields and toss her back towards home. Cup put her head down to brace herself against the wind that was tring and tried to stop her from getting to school. She finally made it to the wall of the playground. She was still about a half hour early, so she rested in the shelter of the wall.

At least it'll be to my back on the way home, she thought. She took a bottle of milk from her bag and took a few mouthfuls. In the howl of the wind she thought she heard another sound. She listened harder. Yes, a weak whine came from the scrub nearby.

She left her bag and crept across to have a look. She could hear nothing. Yet something inside her told her that her ears had been right.

'I'm Cup. I'd like to help you,' she said.

The whining started again; it was coming from inside the scrub. She pulled the foliage back. A large burrow opened before her eyes. Feathers and fox fur clung to the briars at its mouth. There were fox-paw tracks on the fresh earth. It was dark inside. She looked into the grey blackness, and waited.

All kinds of thoughts came to mind. One thing she knew she must not do was to put her hand in there, a fox would think she was attacking, and could bite her. More whines came from the inside. She peered closer. She could see something moving.

She reached out and touched it. It was a living thing. It was a fox cub, very weak; its eyes not yet open. She picked it up. It snuggled its nose to Cup and stuck out its tongue. Your mom or dad must have gone for food and not come back, Cup thought.

Another whine came from the burrow. Yes, a second cub. Cup picked it up. Then she remembered she was on her way to school. She took her lunch from her bag, soaked half of it in milk and fed them. They shook their little heads. Cup laughed at the way they crinkled their noses and stuck out their tongues. They were so hungry that they sucked the wet food off her fingers.

'I'll give you some more later,' she promised and replaced them as far as she could reach into the burrow.

There were no children in the schoolyard. Cup went around to the front; only one car was parked outside. She was blown towards the front door, where she bumped into the Principal.

'Good heavens, child, where are you going?'

'Sorry, Mrs Martin, it's the wind. It got hold of me and . . . here I am,' Cup held onto her.

'School is closed; half the roof is gone,' Mrs Martin said. She pointed at the broken tiles strewn around the front yard.

'I'd better be off home so,' Cup said.

'I'll take you home; that wind will pick you up like a paper bag,' Mrs Martin took her hand.

'Thanks, but I'd like to check on something first.' Cup told her about the fox cubs beyond the school wall, and of her fear that they might have lost their parents.

'It's too dangerous, Cup. What happens if another tile flies off the roof?' Mrs Martin said as she took her arm and led her to the car. On the way home she assured Cup that, with most of her lunch inside them, the fox cubs would be in no danger of starving for at least a day. 'You really love Nature, don't you, Cup?' She asked.

'Yes, there's something new every day.'

'Maybe you'd like to share what you know with your class?'

'If they'd like that, I'd love to, of course!'

'I knew you would. I'll have a word with your teacher,' Mrs Martin smiled and patted Cup's hand.

Cup relaxed; happy that she had found somebody who was on her side; who understood her.

CHAPTER 11

THE FIGHT WITH JACK-THE-BEAR

Cup was surprised to see Kee-Kee waiting in the kitchen with Mrs Hewitt when she got home.

'She just kept flapping at the windows until I let her in,' Mrs Hewitt said.

Kee-Kee had no time for conversation. She landed on Cup's right shoulder and cackled every sound she knew. Up and down she hopped: flap - flap of wings.

'Kee-Kee, calm down. Please tell me what's going on,' Cup pleaded. The bird snuggled her silky head to Cup's neck.

'It's Jack-the-Bear, the chainsaw man. He's back in the forest. I must go there now,' Cup said to Mrs Hewitt, and ran out the door. A whoosh of wind blew her across the yard and into the field.

By the time Mrs Hewitt found her voice Cup was flying through the gap into the forest. Kee Kee pointed her beak towards the danger; Cup raced on. In the distance she heard what she feared: the whining moan of the chainsaw. She ran towards the noise. Kee-Kee still clung to her. The thumpy-thump-thump of the bird's little heart made her race even faster. As Cup got closer to the noise, Kee-Kee crouched low on her shoulder. Then she cawed and flew ahead of Cup.

Strange, Cup thought, as Kee-Kee did a somersault in the air and flew off towards the noise. She wondered what could make a bird, who was so scared of a chainsaw, fly to where one was working. She soon found out.

She had to stop and catch her breath at the sight that met her. A battle raged under an elm tree. On the ground Jack-the-Bear was swinging the chainsaw at a pair of dive-bombing birds. As he swung and roared the saw, Cup thought he looked just like a spaceman; he wore a helmet with a window in front to let him look out and a bright yellow suit that seemed to be all one piece; tucked right down into black Wellington boots. As she watched, Tok kept diving at his face and Kee-Kee flew around him just out of reach of his wild swings. He threw the saw on the ground when Cup rushed at him.

'Are you crazy, lass? I could've cut your head off,' he said as he removed his helmet.

'Like you want to cut the heads off my birds?' Cup said

angrily. Tok and Kee-Kee took a breather overhead on a branch of the elm.

'I've got work to do; what the hell are you lot up to?' He took a step towards Cup. She didn't move. For a moment he stood there looking down at her. Cup stared up at him; not blinking. It was as if she was reading what was going on inside his head. Something about her eyes made him stop and think. He scratched his head. The chainsaw motor ticked over on the ground. Slowly he squatted down. He had to go on one knee and sit back on his heel and lean down to bring his eyes level with hers.

On the branch Tok said, '*tok – wawr*' and Kee-Kee said, '*caw – cawr.*' Cup looked at Jack-the-Bear as if to say that her troops were ready for battle again, if he so wished. The man looked at the birds. He scratched his head and brought his eyes back to Cup. Her eyes looked straight at him; straight and steady.

'What do you want?' he asked.

'We want you to stop cutting down perfectly good trees,' she answered. She folded her arms and watched as his mouth opened and closed.

No words came out. He pointed at her. The finger seemed to be as thick as her arm. She tried not to notice. He shaped his fingers into a fist and stood up. 'We? That's you, and who else?' he sneered.

Cup looked at the birds. Tok spread his wings. He looked like a great black eagle.

Jack-the-Bear threw back his head and laughed.

Cup turned and went to the base of the elm. By then it was already cut halfway through. She picked up a fistful of sawdust and rubbed it between her fingers. It had the fresh clean feel of a healthy tree. She held it to her nose. She closed her eyes at the tangy scent of fresh elm. There was no smell of disease or colour of decay.

She saw Jack-the-Bear putting on his helmet. He pulled down the visor. She leaned back against the tree. He picked up the chainsaw and squeezed the trigger. The engine roared into life. The chainsaw came closer and closer to the tree. The noise hurt Cup's ears.

They stood facing each other; a big man armed with a chainsaw, a little girl completely without fear. He tried to put the saw to the tree. Kee-Kee and Tok dived and flew at his face. The man released the saw to save himself with his hands. Cup wrenched the saw away from the tree. It felt much heavier than herself. She had to drop it.

He picked up the saw again and revved it right in her face, trying to frighten her. She had to close her eyes.

'Get out of my way,' he roared.

She didn't move. He then threw her aside as if she was a doll and placed the saw back into the cut. She ran at him. He was crouched over the roaring saw. Cup jumped on his back and beat at him with her fists. He shrugged.

She ripped off his helmet. It was so heavy that it almost

knocked her off his back. She let it fall on the ground. He pulled the saw from the tree and swung it around. She took a grip of his hair and held on. Kee-Kee dived down and scratched at his face.

Tok flew down, grabbed the helmet in his claws and flew high up into the trees. Jack-the-Bear and Cup looked on, amazed.

'Do you know what that helmet cost me? Nearly as much as the saw.' He grabbed a light branch, broke it and threw it up at Tok.

Cup wondered how Tok could be so strong. The heaviest thing she'd seen him carry up to this was a wheel of a bicycle. Now he flew over the treetops above them as if the helmet was no heavier than a stocking. Though the wind up there was strong, he just spread his wings and soared on top of it with the helmet. Jack-the-Bear kicked at the ground and cursed. Cup hopped down off his back.

'That there tree's got Dutch elm disease; it has to come down,' he roared.

'Who told you that? It has no more disease than your helmet,' Cup said.

She remembered that day when Tok and Kee-Kee led her to this very tree. The men had carved number 67 down low at its base. If this tree was supposed to have Dutch elm disease, then all the 66 others had a meeting with a chainsaw in their futures as well.

'You know well that there's nothing wrong with that tree,' Cup argued.

Jack-the-Bear scratched his head and said nothing.

'If you get away with cutting this one down, what then?' She placed her hands on her hips.

'I'm only doing what I'm told.'

'By whom? Who tells you to kill good trees?'

'Kill! I know what I'll kill!' he pointed at her.

'No you won't,' she said. 'I know all about you.'

Cup remembered the men and their jeep. She described them to him. He shook his head. Then she told him the registration number of the jeep. She mentioned their chatting about furniture and chairs and boats. He was about to hit her. She did not flinch. His hand paused, and returned to rub the stubble on his face.

'There are more trees marked for cutting, aren't there? Cup asked.

'Nope.' He waved his hands.

'So you think you're clever?' She smiled.

Tok flew down and perched beside Kee-Kee. The man put his hands to his head. Cup beckoned him over and showed him the number, 67 carved into the base of the tree.

'How'd you know about this?' he hissed.

'I have friends; I know everything that goes on in this forest,' Cup said.

'You know . . . everything that goes . . . ?' He picked up

the light branch and broke it again. He grabbed its branches and ripped them from the stem. 'Are you going to get lost and let me get on with my work?' he asked, almost politely.

'Are you going to get lost and leave elm 67 to heal itself?' Cup asked.

After what seemed like ages he strode across to his van and picked up his mobile phone. He dialled in a number. Tok and Kee-Kee landed on a branch just out of his reach. He swiped at them, but they took no notice. Cup strolled across in time to pick up the gist of his phone conversation.

'A protest, yes.' He was saying. 'How many?' He looked from Cup to the birds. 'Well there's a girl . . . three, yes, three altogether.' He winced and held the phone away from his ear. 'No; they're not letting me continue,' he said. A pause while he listened. 'Yes, I know all about the contract.' Another pause. 'No; hardly half way through the first one when they stopped me.' Cup could hear a shrill voice rasping from the phone. 'That's what I'm telling you, not one, nothing at all, yet,' he said.

'I'm out of here,' he said as the phone call ended. For a long time he looked from Cup to the birds. 'You're going to cost me my job,' he said as he put the phone back in the van.

Cup watched as Jack-the-Bear walked back to the tree, picked up the saw and put on the safety catch. The birds let him know they weren't sad to see him go as he got into the van with the saw. He wound down the window and looked at the three of them.

'You win, for now,' he said, 'but we'll be back tomorrow with machinery that you can't stop.' He started the van. Even the birds grimaced at the foul-smelling smoke from the engine.

CHAPTER 12

THIEVES IN THE NIGHT

'It cannot be right,' Mrs Hewitt agreed after she'd listened to Cup's story of the fight in the forest with Jack-the Bear. 'The problem is,' she added, 'what can we do about it?'

For a while they were both silent as they looked out the kitchen window towards the forest. It was almost dark, but the storm was easing.

'Those clouds will open tomorrow; always pours after a storm,' Mrs Hewitt said.

'Is there a law against it?' Cup asked.

'Against the rain?' Mrs Hewitt teased. 'Of course I know what you mean, Cup. What time is it? I think I have an idea.'

Mrs Hewitt had remembered an old friend of hers, a retired judge. Soon she was talking to him on the phone, telling him the whole story. She then handed the phone over to Cup.

'They're going to cut down 60 elm trees, maybe more,' Cup said to the judge.

'Do you have their names?' Judge Moore asked.

She gave him the name of Jack-the-Bear and the registration number of the jeep. He told her that permission was needed to cut down trees in a public forest but that Dutch elm disease would be a good reason to allow it. Cup said she didn't think there was Dutch elm disease in the forest; the sawdust was soft and there were leaves on the trees. Judge Moore said he would do what he could to get the law-and-order people on to it. It would take a little time to check everything out; the weekend would slow things down, so he advised Cup to keep up her watch on the trees in the meantime.

'But there are only three of us; maybe four if Mrs Hewitt joins in,' Cup said, looking over at Mrs Hewitt.

'I'm sure she will,' he said. There was a slight pause. 'By the way, Cup,' Judge Moore asked. 'Who taught you all you know about the forest.'

'Old Mr Acorn . . . and my birds,' she replied.

'Acorn? Did you say Acorn?' the Judge asked.

'Yes,' Cup replied. 'Why do you ask?'

'Mr Acorn was my best friend. I miss him,' the Judge said sadly.

'I miss him too,' Cup said.

'I'll do everything I can to help. I promise you that,' Judge Moore said before wishing her luck and hanging up.

'Tom . . . Mr Hewitt gets home tonight, Cup' Mrs Hewitt said. 'We will need to talk to him.'

They both thought this over for a moment. Then, as if with one mind, they heated up the oven and, together, began to make brown bread and scones. While these were baking, Mrs Hewitt suggested that they should try to get a photographer to be there in the morning.

'People who are up to mischief don't like having pictures of it in the newspapers,' she said. 'And I think you should tell that nice Mrs Martin all about it,' she added as Cup turned the bread in the oven.

'Mrs Martin!' Cup said.

'Trust me, Cup. She seems just like a lady who'd want to know all about this,' Mrs Hewitt said.

She was right. After hearing the story from Cup Mrs Martin promised to come around to the house that evening to meet them. Now would be a good time to get Cup's classmates involved, Mrs Martin thought. After calling around to the class teacher and phoning the parents she drove to the Hewitts'. She arrived just as Mr Hewitt finished his meal. They had a long discussion about what they were going to do and all agreed to meet at 8.00 next morning at the edge of the forest.

Cup went to bed early. She was very tired after the fight with Jack-the-Bear and soon was deep in sleep. Sometime during the night Kee-Kee woke her by pulling at her hair and slapping her face with her wings. It was dark and quiet. Kee-Kee cackled to hurry her out of slumber land.

'You flew in a window, didn't you?' Cup said as she slid down the ladder and ran to the Hewitts' bedroom. She told them that something was happening in the forest. Mrs Hewitt guessed as much when she saw the excited antics of Kee-Kee on Cup's shoulder. The bird wanted out of there as if the place was on fire.

'Its too late, Cup and it's too dangerous,' Mr Hewitt said, sleepily.

'I don't care. I just have to go.'

Mr and Mrs Hewitt knew there would be no stopping her. Mr Hewitt gave her his torch and said that she could go ahead while he was rounding up everybody else. They would follow her into the forest almost immediately.

'If something is happening, stay out of sight, Cup until we get there,' he pleaded.

'I will,' Cup said rushing out of the room.

'Promise,' he called after her.

'I promise,' she shouted back as she went out the front door.

By the time Cup reached the forest her eyes had adjusted to the darkness. Heavy rain poured from a sky of black clouds. She held on to Kee-Kee's legs so as to be sure where to go. She wondered what was happening. There was no chainsaw sound. Still Kee-Kee flew on. Cup noticed that they were not going towards elm 67 but instead, followed a narrow pathway down towards the river. After a while she saw some bright lights through the trees a little way ahead.

They moved with care along the path that led them to the lights. There was still no sight or sound of Tok. A set of headlamps showed Jack-the-Bear and another man trying to start a chainsaw. It spluttered to a short roar, then died each time. Cup moved carefully through undergrowth to get around behind the lights. It was the same jeep as before. The back door was open. In the beam of the headlights, the rain looked like a waterfall.

The chainsaw spluttered, roared, gasped for air and came to life again. Cup crept underneath the jeep and then climbed up into the cab through the side door. She switched on Mr Hewitt's torch and began looking at all the wires under the steering wheel. She pulled out the wires of the horn and twisted them together. Suddenly the horn started blaring and the noise was almost as loud as the saw. She then started frantically pulling out more wires until the lights died. She switched off the torch. The saw stopped whirring. She could hear voices shouting, coming closer. In the darkness, the horn sounded as if it was calling the dead from their graves.

She slipped out of the cab and back into the undergrowth. The man with Jack-the-Bear stumbled towards the jeep, like he was blindfolded. He twisted and turned knobs and switches. Still the horn called out. The lights stayed off. Cup stole further into the undergrowth towards the elm tree. There she saw the shapes of Tok and Kee-Kee on a branch.

Jack-the-Bear left the saw on the ground behind the tree and went over to the jeep. The horn was getting weaker now. He opened the bonnet. Cup ran to the tree and pulled the saw up along the path. Tok and Kee-Kee soon joined her.

Tok wrapped his claws around the handle and tried to fly with it. It was too heavy but he was still able to help Cup move the saw along. Soon they reached a clearing.

'It's all right, Tok; we'll hide it somewhere here,' Cup panted. At first Tok would not listen. He spread his wings and tried to rise into the air with the heavy saw. Kee-Kee tried to help but they soon realised that Cup's plan was better. Dawn had turned the sky to grey.

Cup crept back along the path. The horn no longer sounded. The men seemed to be trying to start the jeep. The engine didn't seem to know about it. It just gave a little groan, like it was being called too early in the morning. They banged down the bonnet. While Jeep-Man took out his mobile phone, Jack-the-Bear walked back towards the tree. He reached down behind it for his saw, searching the spot where he'd left it. He went on his knees and had a closer look all around.

In a moment he was back on his feet.

'First my helmet, now my saw!' he roared as he kicked the tree. Tok and Kee-Kee flew in a circle overhead. This time they landed on the topmost branch.

It was getting much brighter. The men waited in the jeep. Cup could see the glow of their cigarettes as they sheltered in the cab from the rain. Cup knew that they must have called for help. She knew it was time to get the others. Before leaving she checked for a number at the base of the elm. With her fingers she found the drill hole. Just above it she traced # 98.

She stole back along the path until she was well out of sight of the men. Then she ran. Two photographers waited at the edge of the forest. They said Mrs Hewitt had sent them ahead and she would be there soon. Cup told them about the jeep and led them back to the spot where they could get pictures of the two men sitting in it without being seen. Tok still kept watch on the treetop, but Cup couldn't see Kee-Kee anywhere.

Once they had the pictures they wanted they half-walked half-ran all the way back. By then the Hewitts were waiting with Mrs Martin and Judge Moore. He smiled at Cup. The photographers got them all into a group for a photograph.

Just before the cameras flashed, Kee-Kee flew onto Cup's shoulder.

'Poser,' she teased as Kee-kee snuggled into her.

Cup then took everybody to see the tree she now called elm 67. Mrs Martin laughed when Cup told her how she'd stopped Jack-the-Bear from cutting completely through it. 'You were very brave,' Judge Moore said.

'You have amazing power over these birds,' Mrs Martin said, stroking Kee-Kee. She looked at her watch and back along the path.

'It's like she's their mother,' the Hewitts added.

'They're the ones with the power. Sometimes they seem to know what I'm thinking . . .' The photographers took a picture of Cup pointing at the gash in the tree. 'Even before I think it,' she added, startled by the flash.

Just as she said that, Kee-Kee flew off. Cup explained that Tok was half-a-mile away keeping watch on his own at elm 98. Judge Moore said that the Inspectors from the Forestry Department would be there soon. Mr Hewitt suggested that they should divide their resources. He asked if anybody had a mobile phone; Mrs. Martin was making a call on hers, the photographers had another, and Judge Moore another. Mr Hewitt said he and Mrs Martin would stay by elm 67; that Judge Moore and one of the photographers would go back to the edge of the forest and wait for the inspectors; and that

Cup, Mrs Hewitt and the other photographer would go to elm 98.

Just then Kee-Kee suddenly arrived back. Her excited cackle told Cup that something was happening. Kee-Kee flew off again, Cup almost flying with her. Cameras flashed. The photographer followed with Mrs Hewitt.

They reached the clearing out of breath. Stooping down they could see a lot of activity going on. This time it looked serious. From the path near elm 98 they saw a tractor towing away the jeep. Another jeep waited nearby as well as a big yellow machine, like a combine-harvester, that had a huge, circular saw-blade on an arm in front of it. A driver revved the engine of the harvester. A *Dinosaw*, Cup thought, as the arm folded up and out, making the machine move like a dinosaur. The saw started turning; faster and faster. The driver tested the blade on a bush. A quick gnash of its teeth and it was through it like a hot knife through ice cream.

Jack-the-Bear came out from behind the *Dinosaw* and walked ahead of it to elm 98. He gripped a slash hook in his hands.

Cup jumped out and ran out to meet him.

'Don't, Cup. Its too dangerous,' Mrs Hewitt screamed. It was too late. Cup was between him and the tree. For a moment everything stopped, except the rain.

Tok and Kee-Kee flew around and around the neck of the machine and then onto a branch of the elm. Pigeons, wood-sparrows, rooks, robins, thrushes, wrens, blackbirds, kestrels, a lone raven, even an owl, all took their perches in the trees roundabout; squawking and screeching in alarm. Jack-the-Bear stepped to one side. Cup did the same. He took a step towards her. She didn't move.

'You're wasting our time, little lass,' he growled. He leaned on the slash hook and bent towards her.

'You're doing this all by yourselves! Aren't you?' Cup said. 'You don't have any permission to cut down the trees. You're thieves and tree-killers.'

'Get out of my way, girl,' Jack-the-Bear said.

The engine of the *Dinosaw* revved; the blade of the saw whined. It sounded like a dragon in full fury. Tok flew onto the bonnet of the *Dinosaw*. The driver shouted at him. Tok ripped off the wiper of the cab window with his beak, flew off and dropped it in the light branches at the top of the elm.

Kee-Kee flew down and perched on the neck of the *Dinosaw*; just above the whizzing saw. Jack-the-Bear swiped at her with the slash hook. She saw it coming and flew further up the neck, where she started attacking something black with her beak on the underswide, like she'd attacked the knots on the broken clothesline last year.

The *Dinosaw* drove towards Cup. She didn't move. She could see right under the monster. If she crouched a little it could drive over her without touching her. She felt a hand on her shoulder. Mrs Hewitt took a tight grip on her soggy coat and stood beside her. A camera flashed; and flashed again.

The driver jumped out of the cab. He swung a big hammer at the photographer. 'Give me that camera,' he shouted. The hammer missed and the photographer ran.

Mrs Hewitt gasped. Jack-the-Bear gave her a close-up view of the blade of the slash hook.

'Don't move,' Cup whispered.

'I was about to say the same,' Mrs Hewitt said.

'Move, or we'll knock your heads off,' both men roared. An exchange of cackles between the birds sent Kee-Kee flying towards elm 67. It was time to get help. Tok took over the attack on the black thing in the neck of the *Dinosaw*. Cup, dodging past the slash-hook, took a closer look. She could see two black hoses, like big black worms, running all the way underneath the arm to the saw. To the birds it was the only soft thing they could attack on the machine.

The driver of the *Dinosaw* was making a phone call. He hopped and roared with anger. Cup thought he'd eat the little phone.

'We just have to hang on for a few minutes,' Cup whispered.

'How do you know?' Mrs Hewitt asked wiping the rain off her face.

'Kee-Kee has gone to get help.'

The phone call ended. The driver shouted at Jack-the-Bear who stretched out his arms and with a roar picked Cup and Mrs Hewitt up and threw them in the bushes beside the track, as if they were twigs. The *Dinosaw* roared towards elm 98. The photographer came back. He ran in front of the harvester and tried to take a picture. The driver swung the arm and knocked him aside.

'He's broken my phone and camera!' the photographer wailed, unable to get up.

Jack-the-Bear stood over the ladies but for a moment his attention was distracted by the harvester. In the twinkle of an eye Cup ran past him. He raced after her, followed a little more slowly by Mrs Hewitt.

Meanwhile Tok had switched his attack to the driver in the cab of the machine. He knocked the man's helmet off. In one swoosh it flew out the window. The driver stopped the machine. Tok flew in one window again, ripped off his goggles, and flew out the other. The driver rushed after him. Jack-the-Bear made a swipe at Tok with the slash hook. He missed. The blade whistled through the air and hit the driver on the shoulder. It cut right through leather and padding, and bruised his skin.

Jack-the-Bear helped him back into the cab. The engine roared. Tok returned to the neck of the harvester and ripped and tore at the black tubes.

'We'll wrap ourselves around the tree,' Mrs Hewitt said.

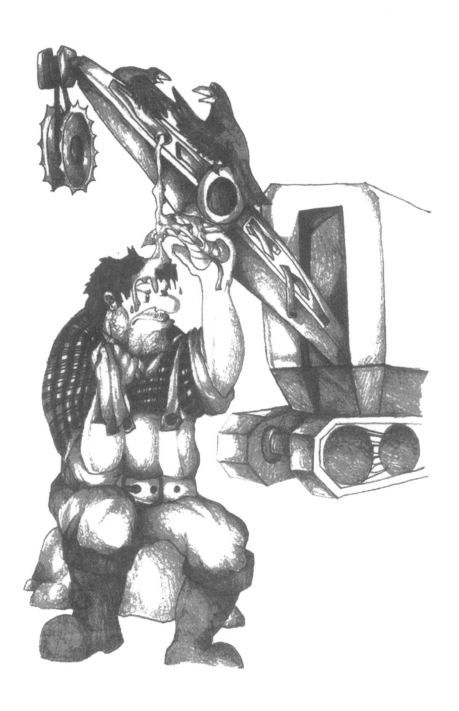

'And hold each other's hands.'

Cup went behind the tree. Mrs Hewitt gripped her hands from the front.

'Hold on tight,' they told each other as Jack-the-Bear tried to pull them apart. The driver inched the *Dinosaw* closer to the tree. The long neck reached out. Cup looked up as the blade lowered into position near the top of Mrs Hewitt's hat. She also saw that another raven had joined Tok in his battle with the tubes.

'Not yet; too high up,' Jack-the-Bear shouted as he raised a hand towards the driver.

'No!' Cup screamed.

Tok swooped down, smack into the man's face. He released his grip on the slash hook and fell backwards. Cup released her hold on Mrs Hewitt. The saw whirled in the air above them. Tok tried to grab the handle of the slash hook. Cup bent down and picked it up for him. Tok wrapped his claws around it and, ducking under the saw, he carried it off over the trees.

'My goodness, how can he do that?' Mrs Hewitt exclaimed.

'You big ugly black thief,' Jack-the-Bear roared. 'I'll shoot you, you robber; I'll fill you with buckshot,' he shouted at the sky as he lay on the ground under the neck of the machine.

Tok's raven-mate glanced after him, then continued attacking the black pipes with even more fury. Suddenly there was a hissing noise and pink liquid dripped down onto Jack-the-Bear. At first he thought they were drops of blood until the driver leapt out of the cab and pointed at the raven. Something that looked like cranberry juice was gurgling from the pipes of the *Dinosaw* and squirting to the ground.

Tok flew back and inspected the work on the pipes. An exchange of cackles with his raven-mate, and they flew around the machine.

'They probably think the red stuff is blood,' Cup said.

'Amazing,' Mrs Hewitt shivered.

The driver threw a spanner at the ravens. It missed and shattered the windscreen of the cab. He dragged himself up into the cab and revved the engine. It roared. He pulled a lever. The great blade whirred again, blowing Mrs Hewitt's hat off her head. Suddenly there was a crunching sound and the blade turned slower and slower; creaking. Then the Dinosaw sighed to a stop, as if apologising for what it had done.

Jack-the-Bear got up and went into the cab. He watched the driver twisting knobs and pulling levers. Another jet of cranberry juice shot from a broken pipe. The saw didn't move. The engine roared, sending up smoke and fumeds.

'What happened to the Dinosaw?' Cup asked.

'That red liquid your birds punctured out of the tubes must be what's needed to turn the saw,' Mrs Hewitt explained, still shaking her head in amazement.

Cup was also amazed that Mrs Hewitt knew about stuff like that.

Tok and his mate perched on a branch of elm 98, just over the heads of the ladies. Tok spread his wings and looked down at Cup.

'Thank you, Tok,' she said.

He seemed to consider her words. For a moment he had a chat with his raven-mate, then hopped down to Cup. For the first time in months he rubbed his head and neck against her face.

'You've grown so strong, even bigger again.' Cup held him and stroked the rough feathers of his neck. *Tok, tok*, he said as he snuggled into her. Then he stiffened, turned his head this way and that, as if listening to something. He climbed onto her head, then up to the branch beside his raven-mate. One look back down at Cup and off he flew towards elm 67, followed by his raven-mate.

'We'd better get back there too,' Mrs Hewitt said.

'This lot can't do any damage for now,' the photographer agreed. 'He might have broken the camera, but the pictures are safe.'

CHAPTER 13

A SURPRISE FOR CUP

On their way back through the forest the rain eased. Soon the sun warmed the dripping trees.

'Please tell them I'm not that badly hurt,' Mrs. Hewitt said when she saw the blue flashing light in the distance near elm 67. She had twisted her ankle on the way and moved slowly with Cup's help. The photographer ran on ahead.

Another yellow steel *Dinosaw* stood silent at the scene. Its neck was folded back against the cab. A pair of ravens and a rook exchanged places on top of it. An ambulance and jeep with a flashing blue light stood near by. Two men ran to meet Mrs Hewitt. Mr Hewitt followed them. They unfolded a stretcher and insisted that she lie on it.

'Did you save the elm?' Cup asked.

Mr Hewitt was a bit distracted; worried about Mrs Hewitt. 'What? Oh . . . they got a couple of branches, but not the tree,' he said, when his wife told him to stop fussing. 'That other teacher and the children were a great help too,' he added.

'Teacher and children?' Cup asked.

'They got here just after the machine,' he pointed towards them in the distance. 'They really messed things up for that machine driver,' he laughed.

Cup looked and saw Mrs Martin talking to a man in uniform. She clapped her hands when she saw the children; about ten of them were guarding the tree with Teacher. Kee-Kee flew shapes overhead, then alighted on Cup's shoulder. A few fast cackles later and she was off again, hovering like when she was learning to fly.

'What's the jeep with the blue light?' Cup asked.

'The Park Ranger and the Forestry Inspectors; the ones Judge Moore called in,' Mr Hewitt said.

Kee-Kee hovered, then clung to the front of Cup's coat. 'It's okay, Kee Kee; I can't hear any chainsaw,' Cup reassured her. Kee-Kee turned her head and looked at where Tok and his raven-mate perched close together.

'I think Cup has a jealous rook on her hands,' Mrs Hewitt laughed.

'You won't mind if I run ahead?' Cup asked Mrs Hewitt.

'I'll be just fine, with all these men fussing around me,' Mrs Hewitt laughed.

As Cup ran towards Teacher and the children some of them ran out to meet her. Every one of the nose-holders was there, including the ones who ripped up her schoolbag. Cup didn't know what to say.

'Can we be friends, Cup?' a girl said.

'Of course you can; you all can,' Cup smiled.

'Mrs Martin told us everything,' a boy said and stroked Kee Kee's feathers.

Mrs Martin joined them. 'Kee-Kee's upset,' Mrs Martin said. 'She knows that your Tok has found a mate.'

Cup looked at the two ravens, perched there at the top of the machine. Though a little sad that she mightn't see much of Tok from now on, she was happy for him.

'He's found his raven-mate,' Cup told everybody. 'They'll make a nest together and have chicks of their own. They'll feed them and teach them all they know.'

'They'll need a huge big nest,' someone said.

'I know exactly where they're going to nest,' Cup said. 'In Jack-the-Bear's huge helmet. Tok's hidden it away somewhere; it'll be just perfect.' She stopped and grabbed Mrs Martin's hand. 'Oh no,' she said, 'the little fox cubs; I forget all about them.'

'They're safe. Their mother came back and took them away,' Mrs Martin assured her.

The Park Ranger insisted that Mrs Hewitt should go to hospital to have her ankle checked out. Mr Hewitt went with her, promising Cup that they'd see her at home later.

'Do you have any idea what you've done, Cup Little?' Mrs Martin asked as she and Judge Moore drove Cup home. Cup just looked at her, wondering what she could have done wrong. 'Do you realise that you've saved 98 elm trees from being turned into furniture and firewood?' She reached across and patted Cup's hand.

'But they'll come again, Mrs Martin. They came in the middle of the night last night,' Cup said.

'Your Tok and Kee-Kee'll have lots of eggs hatched before those people get near a forest again,' Judge Moore said.

'You mean they're going to prison?'

'They'll be doing something a bit more useful, if I have my way,' Judge Moore said sternly. 'Look at all they've done wrong, apart from not having permission to do what they were about to do to the forest: they drove right through Mr Hewitt and me; the attack on you and Mrs Hewitt, and so on. And there are lots of pictures to prove it all.'

'What do you mean, Judge by something useful,' Cup asked.

'I plan to have them do community service. They will spend the next two years planting thousands of young trees instead of cutting down the older ones,' Judge Moore said with a smile.

'That's great, Judge. Old Mr Acorn would be proud of you.' Cup laughed.

'Yes. I think he would,' the Judge agreed.

Mrs Martin brought her car to a stop in Hewitts' yard but kept the engine running.

'You'll come in for tea, won't you?' Cup asked.

'I should be getting home, out of these wet clothes and into a nice bath,' she said.

'There are fruit scones; I baked them myself.'

'Well that's different, isn't it? I wouldn't miss that treat for a hundred baths.'

'Me neither,' Judge Moore said.

While waiting for the kettle to boil Mrs Martin chatted with her about school, the forest and other interests.

'So you're happy here with the Hewitt's,' she asked.

'I dreamed about life being this good,' Cup said as she stood on a chair and poured boiling water into the teapot. She was so busy she hadn't heard the Hewitts' car arriving, nor did she know they had been standing at the door listening to what she'd said.

Mrs Hewitt limped across to her. Cup threw her arms around her and asked about her ankle.

'Nothing that a few days rest won't cure,' she said, and looked towards her husband.

'We're glad you're here, Mrs Martin, and you too, Judge Moore,' he said. 'Because we've something to ask Cup.' All four of them looked at each other and then at Cup. Mr Hewitt sat Cup on the table and seated himself in front of her.

'We'd like to adopt you,' he said to Cup.

'You really mean that?' Cup looked from one to the other.

'You wonderful child, of course we do,' Mrs Hewitt said.

'But only if you'd like to be our family,' Mr Hewitt added.

Cup clung to them both and recited that verse she'd made up in her dreams:

> *'A foster child is just on loan,*
> *This Mom and Dad are not my own.*
> *But if they're seeking love for free,*
> *They'll find it by adopting me.'*

Mrs Martin and Judge Moore agreed to act as sponsors for the adoption, and after that they all tucked into the scones that Cup had made. She was as happy as she had ever been.

On Monday morning, when the carpenters working on the storm-damaged roof finally left, Mrs Martin opened the partitions between the two classrooms of the school for the first time in years. When all the teachers and children were seated she stood up. They hushed as she began to speak.

'This won't take long,' she began. 'One of our pupils, Cup Little will be eleven years old next week. Believe me, she has packed more living into those eleven years than most people fit into twice that time. Her kindness to wildlife and to nature has ensured that a major sin against our forest has been prevented.

To those of you who have held your noses in her presence I assure you that all she smells of is honesty and truth and of everything that is decent in this life. I've brought you all together to share our pride as one of our own students receives a special award from the Forestry and Wildlife Department.

Cup Little, please take your place up here.'

It took Cup a few moments to take it all in. Then she went to each child who'd joined her in the forest and brought them with her. After the applause the Park Ranger made a speech and presented Cup with a scroll. The photographers from the fight in the forest were ready to take more pictures. They smiled at her. The Park Ranger asked Cup if she'd like to say something. She said she would.

Mrs Martin stood her on a chair so that she could be seen. Before she began she whispered something in the Principal's ear. Mrs Martin smiled and then nodded her head.

'The forest is a great place.' Cup began. 'All of the countryside is; the beaches, the rivers, everything. There's something happening all the time, only sometimes it isn't always good. So if we fight for anything, I'd like it to be to make more good things happen.' Cup looked at her friends standing around her. The all nodded, so she bowed and stepped off the chair.

After the applause, Mrs Martin announced that Cup had asked for all of the children in the school to be in the photograph with her.

That weekend Mrs Hewitt was in those corduroy trousers and ready to go to the forest again. She reminded Cup of her promise to tell her how sunset looked from there.

The sun dipped below the horizon in the forest giving back a glow of honeyed amber. Cup and Mrs Hewitt watched wisps of cloud dart across the sky, their underbellies lit up by the light. A thin strip of yellow gilded the horizon until the moon came up to throw silver, shimmering shapes on the waters of the bay.

'This is truly beautiful,' she said.

Cup got a sudden fright when something alighted on her right shoulder. It was Kee-Kee. After rubbing her head to Cup's face she flew back to the top of a tree and perched beside another rook. One said caw and the other cawr before flying away. Kee-Kee has also found a mate, Cup thought. She felt so happy; happy for Kee-Kee; happy for Tok and happy for herself and the Hewitts. She too had a family of her own to be proud of and for the first time friends of her own.

'You don't have to ask my permission every time your friends from school want to visit,' Mrs Hewitt said, as if reading her thoughts.

'And you don't have to fuss about the place being clean enough for them when they come,' Cup smiled, holding her hand tightly as they walked towards home.